One

Love

LANCE

It was a warm weekend in Stoney Brook, Maine. Something that was not common, and that I cherished more and more. "Babe, stop enjoying the sun and make sure we have enough rolls," Billie said, and slapped me on the butt to get my attention.

"It's so nice out. It's never this nice." I closed my eyes and soaked up the morning sun.

"Don't worry, the fog will be back soon." He kissed my cheek as he hurried out of the food truck and back into the restaurant to grab more supplies. We'd met at this very festival three years ago, and since then, so much had changed. The biggest change was Billie, a California native, had moved out here with me. After that, we'd started our own restaurant, and to top it off, the food truck was still going strong.

"It's our anniversary you know." Billie hefted an ice chest into one of the cold storage cabinets.

"Is it? How can you remember that?" I joked and turned away, knowing my smile would give me away.

"Well, it was only the day that you met the one man in Stoney Brook willing to wear a lobster hat while helping you sell your magical lobster rolls. Does that ring a bell?" He leaned against the counter and waited for my answer.

He was just as hot as he was the day we met. Green eyes, dark blond hair, and a smile that I couldn't resist. I moved close to him and rested my hands on his hips. "I don't think anyone has ever worn a lobster hat the way you wear it. Every day and every night, I'm still in awe of you," I whispered as I pressed my lips against his. "Now, if we don't get moving, we won't be able to get our usual spot."

He looked at me and the way his eyes darkened left no doubt, in that moment, the last thing on his mind was working. I shivered as he trailed his lips along my jaw before he pulled back. "You're right, and we cannot be late to feed the masses." He held his hand up for emphasis, of what I wasn't sure, since it kinda resembled an upside-down claw. But it did look dramatic and made me laugh.

We secured the supplies we'd packed the back of the truck and hopped into the front seats.

"Can you believe it's been three years since we met?" Billie asked as he glanced at me.

"Well, some days I feel every minute of it." I leaned back in the seat and focused my attention on the growing foot traffic around us. Casually, I looked over at Billie, whose eyes were boring into the side of my head. "What? I love you. But you have to admit, working together can be challenging at times—not that it's a bad thing." *Fuck, when would I learn to keep my mouth shut?*

His eyes narrowed, and I could practically see the wheels turning as he decided if it was worth a fight or not. "I'm going to ignore that comment as long as you know you'll be making it up to me later."

In the three years we'd been together, I'd learned so much about Billie. He was almost always happy and never started a fight just to fight. But if he was mad, he was mad! And nothing was going to calm him down until his anger ran its course. I'd

Brown Eyed Boy

BL Maxwell

Brown-Eyed Boy

BL Maxwell

Copyright

only seen this once, and I was never so happy, to *not* be the one who had caused it. But I loved him, and if he was upset, I'd do what I could to make him happy. I smiled my best smile at him. The one I knew he couldn't resist. "Baby, I'm sorry. I didn't mean it like that. But you know there've been a few times after working together for twelve hours, when neither one of us had an abundance of patience left."

He smiled then. "Yeah, you're right. You can be a little grouchy sometimes yourself."

"A little?" I wasn't exactly known for my sparkling personality, but Billie was the one every customer made sure to say hello to. "You know, I was practically chasing customers away until I met you. And no, it wasn't the lobster hat. It was you, baby."

He squeezed my leg as I turned off from the main street into the parking lot where we'd set up for the day. "Are your parents still coming this year?" Our families had yet to meet each other, which was what had driven Billie over the edge.

"They said they were, but I'm not going to count on them until I actually see them." It was obvious it hurt him. He was very proud of our restaurant, and he wanted to show it off to his family, who were all a big part of the restaurant business in Sacramento. But so far, they'd cancelled every time they'd made plans. Both of us understood they were busy, but I knew Billie really wanted them to visit.

"We could always fly out there again. I wouldn't mind a few days on the West Coast."

"Sure you wouldn't." He saw right through me, like he always did. "We're just a little busy with the festivals."

I pulled the truck into the same spot we'd parked at every year we'd done the Tall Ships Festival together. Billie stood up and got ready to get to work, but before he could get too far, I was up and standing in front of him. "You know I love you, right? Because no way in hell anyone else would put up with me, and you're kinda wonderful."

He laughed and kissed me. "I love you too. Now let's do this. You know we're going to have a line as soon as we open."

His words put me in motion, and I got busy setting up the food trays and organizing all the sides and desserts. We'd added a few items that Billie had wanted to try and see how they'd sell. Of course, they all did well. We still had a simple menu, but we rotated a few of those other items with the lobster rolls and loaded fries.

"I'm excited to see how the lobster tacos do," Billie said.

"Oh, they're going to be a huge hit. I wouldn't be surprised if they outsell the lobster rolls." I double-checked we had the rolls ready, and the fresh tortillas we'd made last night. "Hopefully, the taco truck doesn't mind the competition." A little competition was good. The year after we'd met and done so well with my original lobster rolls, there were two other trucks selling something similar. But there was room for everyone, and we all had slightly different food, so Billie and I both welcomed the challenge of making quality products that were unique and delicious. So far, we'd done okay.

"Do you think so? The original rolls do so well, that's a lot of competition."

"I do, and we can use the slaw on them." I'd worked hard to perfect those lobster rolls, but Billie had helped make them even better.

"I like that they're a little taste of California. With the lobster, there's a little of us both in them." He stacked the tortillas while he spoke, and I grinned at him. When he noticed, he tossed a still frozen fry in my direction.

"Hey, we might need that."

He smiled at me and stepped closer, his hands on my hips this time. "One fry?" he murmured, and just like that I was caught under his spell. "Do you really think we'll miss it?" He leaned in and lightly blew across my neck.

"Oh god, Billie!" I gripped his shoulders and pushed him back enough to meet his eyes, and to give me a second to get myself under control.

"What?" he asked, all angelic and wide-eyed innocence. But I knew exactly how innocent he wasn't.

"It's time to open up." He smiled at me before shoving the lobster hat on his head and stepping out the door. "We'll be finishing this later," he called through the order window as he tapped his fingers on the counter. A line was already formed, so he did what he did best and started selling them our food. "I know you heard me."

"Oh, I heard you, and I consider that a promise," I yelled back at him.

His eyes locked on mine for a full second before he bent over laughing, making the claws on the hat flap around on his head. When he finally got himself together again, he ran to the end of the line of customers and started taking orders. I was putting down some fries and getting a few orders organized when he came in, took my hand, and slapped a stack of orders in it. "I promise." He rushed away to greet more people and, just like every day we spent together, he made it all better.

Two

All Work

BILLIE

"Are we ready to go?" I asked as Lance did his last check, making sure everything was secured and ready to go.

"Yep, and I'm so glad we have everything already prepped for tomorrow." He slid into the driver's seat and drove cautiously through the lingering crowd.

"Do you think tomorrow will be as busy?" I asked.

"Should be. I mean, it's been the same for the past three years. You know that." Lance grinned at me and squeezed my hand.

"Yep, always busy." I looked out the passenger side, not wanting to spoil my news until we got home and bit the inside of my cheek to make sure of it.

I worked hard, but Lance worked *hard*! He was one of the most driven people I'd ever met. But he did it in a way that never made me feel like I was second to his work. I loved him. God, I loved him so much. And because of that, I wanted to surprise him. He was so fucking hard to surprise. He worked all the time, but he was so freaking observant that nothing got past him.

He pulled the truck in behind the restaurant and next to the stairway that led to our apartment. "Help me bring everything up, then we can get to bed early if you want," Lance said.

"That sounds great. Maybe a shower first?" I asked. Then I nearly walked right into him as he stopped halfway through the door and turned to face me.

"*Only* a shower?" His eyes smoldered, and he smirked. There was no way in hell I was going to disagree. I shifted the supplies I was carrying enough to wrap one arm around his waist and kiss his neck.

"When have we ever *only* had a shower?" It was true; anytime the two of us showered together, it didn't end up saving us any time. Not that either of us minded.

Lance kissed me softly before turning to lead me to the kitchen, where we both set down the supplies we'd carried in. After everything was packed away, neither of us moved, both locked into each other's gaze as the heat grew between us.

A smile spread on Lance's lips right before he bolted for the bathroom, tearing his shirt off as he crossed the threshold. His pants soon followed as he hopped around, trying to get them off while turning on the water. I walked slowly toward him as he started laughing and flinging his foot all over, trying to disengage the leg of his pants. He was so preoccupied that when he finally looked up, I was right in front of him.

"You weren't going to start without me, were you?" I asked and pulled my own shirt off. Lance stopped what he was doing to stare at my chest.

"Oh god no," he whispered before stepping into my arms. "You feel so good."

There was something so hot about his bare chest pressed against mine while his dick hardened against my leg. Somehow, I managed to get naked without too much hopping around. And with a little help from Lance, we relaxed under the warm water. Neither of us spoke as we slowly kissed and took the time to explore each other's bodies. My fingers played along the planes of his stomach as his lips traced the side of my neck. "What do you want, baby?" I whispered as I gripped him. "I'll give you anything you ask for."

His breath sped up as I slowly stroked him, and his hips started to move. "You," he groaned. "I just want you."

I spun him around and his hands automatically went to the wall of the enclosure. Reaching for the bottle of lube we kept handy, I quickly got him ready. As I pressed into him, it felt like the first time all over again, only better. Both of us fought for control as he pushed back against me, and I tried to hold his hips and drive into him. It was intense and heady with emotions, and neither of us was ready for it to end when I felt Lance tighten around me as he found his release.

The sounds he made as he chased those sensations were enough to drive me over the edge. I pulled him close to my chest, both of us panting as we tried to come back down. "I love you," I whispered in his ear.

"I love you too," he mumbled, already fading from the long day.

"Come on, baby, let's get to bed." We both helped each other dry off and in just a few minutes we were lying in bed ready to get some much-needed sleep. "Lance? I have a surprise for you." I hadn't meant to say it, but I couldn't wait any longer.

"Wha—?" he mumbled.

"Remember how your great-great-grandfather came here from Ireland and met your great-great-grandmother?"

He cracked an eye open but didn't move. "Yeah?"

"Well, I might have booked us a trip to Dublin, so you can see exactly where he grew up." I braced for his reaction, hoping it wasn't bad.

His eyes opened wide, and he sat up. "Are you kidding?"

"No, not kidding."

His smile grew as he tackled me to the bed before kissing me. "You're serious?"

"Yes." I laughed. "You always talk about going there and visiting the town he grew up in. We have a week off after this weekend. I booked it, and I found someone who might be a relative."

"No, you did not," he said, now fully awake.

"Oh, I did. Your mom and I have been looking through your genealogy and we found someone who still lives there."

"Who is it?"

"His name is Joseph Moran, and he's in his sixties, but he owns a little business there. Your mom has talked to him quite a bit since we found him. I hope you don't mind. I booked us a room at a hotel in Castlecomer, where he lives."

"Why would I mind? I'm thrilled. Thanks, Billie, you know I've always wanted to travel, but you also know I hate taking time off work. Thanks for doing this." He brushed his thumb against my cheek and the look in his eyes told me more about his heart than any of his words ever could.

"You have no idea how relieved I am. I thought you'd be happy, but like you said, you don't like to take time off. Maybe we can start mapping out where we want to go while we're there?"

"That sounds great. I need to check my passport and find someone to cover our shifts. What about the bread orders?" He sat bolt upright in bed, as he went over his list of things he'd need to do to feel good about leaving our business.

"I took care of it. Your mom asked her employees if anyone would be willing to help out. She's going to cook and have two people from her restaurant help her. I think she's actually excited about it."

"We're going to Ireland!" he said with a nod and a faraway look in his eyes.

"We are. Now let's get some sleep, so we're not both worthless tomorrow." He snuggled in close to my side, and after one more kiss, we both slept.

Three
Fireworks

LANCE

Sunday flew by, and since both of us were ready for the festival to be over, neither of us was too upset when we sold out about an hour before closing time. Some vendors left early, but there was no way I was going to let this night pass without spending some time watching the fireworks.

"Babe, can you get those two bags there?" I asked Billie when he walked in from bringing in the sign and closing up out front.

"Yeah, are we going up top?" he asked with a grin that lit up those beautiful eyes.

"Of course we are. It wouldn't be the Tall Ships Festival without our regular tradition of enjoying the fireworks." After double-checking everything was wiped down and put away, Billie and I walked around the side of the truck. I carried up the chairs and a blanket, while he carried the food.

"I thought we sold out?" he asked as he peeked inside once we were both settled by the giant lobster perched on top of the truck.

"It's a tradition. No way were we not having lobster rolls and fries while we watch the fireworks."

He kissed my cheek before doling out the food and after we settled in, both of us ate in comfortable silence. I wasn't sure how many lobster rolls I'd eaten in my lifetime, but it was a lot. And these were some of the best, even if I did say so myself.

The fireworks started with a single rocket lighting up the sky above us and illuminating the masts of the tall ships that were anchored just offshore. It was beautiful, and when Billie snuggled in close to me, I was once again so fucking glad he'd gone on that road trip.

"What are you thinking on so hard over there, Mr. Karl?" Billie asked as he rested his head on my shoulder.

"Just saying thanks to whoever it was that put you on that road trip and helped you end up here."

"I think even if we hadn't met when we did, eventually we would have found our way to each other." He snuggled in closer, and I laid my hand over his. The fireworks were beautiful, but for a while all I could see was Billie, and when he caught me staring, he shook his head before pulling me in for a kiss. "I love you," he murmured.

When the show was over, we made our way back to the apartment like we had every year, but when we made love that night, I couldn't seem to get enough of his touch. He was everything to me, and I decided right then and there that I needed to show him how much I appreciated everything he'd done since we'd met. I drifted off to visions of us working together in some faraway restaurant, and like always, we worked together like a well-oiled machine.

"Good morning, sleepy head," I said as I settled a tray of food on the nightstand next to Billie and kissed him on the forehead.

His eyes cracked open as he struggled to take in what was happening. "What's all this?" he asked.

"I made you breakfast in bed. I thought you could use some pampering."

He took a bite of a piece of bacon and grinned at me. "Oh, I could always use some pampering. But you didn't need to go to all this trouble. I love to watch you cook."

It was true. He'd sit at one of the stools on the other side of the island and watch as I cooked. I couldn't count how many recipes we'd perfected or dumped over the years using this same method. "Sorry, babe. But you'll just have to force your-self to enjoy eating breakfast and not worry about critiquing it today."

He laughed and pulled the tray over to his lap. "Come here and join me. I want to share breakfast with my boyfriend before we go to work." He patted the bed next to him and for the next thirty minutes, we caught up on what we'd be working on through the day and touched on what plans had been made for Ireland.

"We're really going?" I asked again. It still hadn't sunk in, and since last night I'd probably asked him twenty times or more.

"We're really going. And we're going to have such a good time. You know my family is from Scotland, so our ancestors were practically neighbors," Billie said around a big bite of eggs.

"You never told me that before. Are we going to Scotland too?" I knew the two countries were close, but I wasn't sure *how* close.

"Not this time. I figure we can do that on another trip. I want to focus on your ancestor on this trip. Alice has a lot of information about him and your great-great-grandmother."

"I remember when I was a kid, she was really into genealogy for a while. Well, in between running a restaurant and raising kids. I'm amazed she had any time to have a hobby."

"I'm amazed *you* have time for a hobby," Billie said to me.

"What hobby?" I knew for a fact I had no time for hobbies, and since Billie and I had been together, we either spent time together at work or plotting new ideas for the restaurant or food truck. But we didn't do much else, other than the food tours he'd helped promote in the downtown area.

"Food? I mean, you're always working on new recipes or perfecting the ones you have. How many lobster roll recipes did you try? If you think about it, cooking is not only your job, it's also your hobby," Billie said from the bathroom where he'd just finished brushing his teeth.

"Well, I guess you could be right. It is what I love, and it's what we need to do to stay ahead of the competition."

"What competition? You've got the lobster roll business locked in. Now we can hit them with the new recipes we talked about." He pulled his pants on and in just a few minutes, we were both ready to go. "Alice is stopping by today to find out if there's anything you need to show her before we leave."

"Thank you so much for asking her to help. You know I wouldn't have wanted to bother her." I wasn't sure why that was, other than we both had too much of a work ethic and even though I was more than willing to help her if I wasn't already swamped, I was always hesitant to ask her for help. Billie had changed all that.

"She asked what she could do to make this trip happen. I think she realizes you need to have some time off, and she also knows you'd never take it off yourself if the decision was left to you." Billie smiled at me, softening the blow of his words. Not that he meant it as an insult, more he'd seen what that drive could do to everyone else involved. It was the very reason he'd left his own family's business and struck out on his own.

"You're amazing," I whispered to him as I kissed his cheek.

"So are you, but if we don't get going, we'll be late, and you'll never live it down if Alice is standing out front waiting with the regulars that you know are going to be there any minute."

"Good thing we don't have a long commute." After locking the door, we jogged down the stairs and right to the back entrance. I flipped all the lights on and made sure we were all set up, Billie opened the door, and with his usual flourish, welcomed everyone in.

Four
Ireland

BILLIE

The plane glided to a landing in Dublin. Not Dublin, California. Dublin, Ireland. I looked past Lance out the window and took note that I was seeing the green of Ireland for the first time in my life. Lance took my hand and squeezed it, but neither of us said a word. The flight had been brutal. We'd tried to sleep for most of it, but I was more than ready to get off the plane and into an actual bed.

"I can't believe we're really here," Lance said while still staring out the window. We were on the ground now, and the airport looked like any other airport to me. But just knowing we were in Ireland gave me a burst of excitement.

"Me either. Now let's hope it doesn't take us too long to go through immigration." We waited forever to get off the plane before following everyone along a long hall that finally led to immigration and customs. The line moved along at a crawl, and the longer I stood, the harder the lengthy flight hit me.

"I'm ready for a nap," Lance mumbled as he thumbed through his documents.

"Me too, but I'm so excited to be here I don't want to miss a second."

"Don't worry, we're going to see every little bit of Ireland possible while we're here." Lance had planned out our trip, and while I was great at planning a menu and implementing it in a restaurant or catering situation, Lance was brilliant when it came to optimizing our time here. He'd mapped it all out, and after a few days in Dublin, and seeing everything we could see of the city, we'd pick up our rental car. He'd planned it so we could have a day or two at each stop along his carefully chosen route, depending on how much there was to see in the area. Originally the plan was to be in Ireland seven days, but when I realized how much there was to see, and how much of it we *wanted* to see, we made sure the restaurant was ready for us to take two weeks off.

"I'm so glad we're not driving today. We can just get a ride to the hotel and sleep a while before we go exploring," I said, as the line inched along.

"The hotel should be close enough we can walk to some of the sites we want to see, and it's also close to the bus stop for the double-decker bus that will take us around Dublin." Lance was so excited, and I knew even though he hadn't mentioned his uncle, he couldn't wait to spend time with him. He'd gone over his recipes trying to find one that he could share with his uncle, and ultimately it came down to his bread. At first, he was going to share his lobster roll recipe, but he wasn't sure how that would go over in Ireland, so he'd packed a jar with some of his personal sourdough starter. Which was huge—he never shared that starter with anyone.

We finally made it through the line, and after getting our passports stamped, we walked out into the airport. There were people everywhere, either arriving, departing, or there to pick up someone. We walked closer to the exit as I tapped on my phone and ordered a car.

"I'm so excited to be here, but I cannot wait to get some sleep in an actual bed," Lance said echoing my earlier thoughts as we stepped outside.

"Same, that flight was pretty brutal." Part of the reason we planned to stay in Dublin for three days was to get our bearings and adjust to the time change, plus we were both excited to see the city. There was so much there and since we'd never been before, we were anxious to see it all. A car pulled up in front of us and an older man stuck his head out the window.

"Billie Watts?"

"That's me," I said, and Lance and I hurried to put our bags in the trunk.

"What brings you two here?" the man asked.

"How do you know we're not locals?" I asked.

"Oh, just a guess," he said with a laugh, and an Irish accent.

"Lance here found a relative in Castlecomer, so we decided we'd come meet him and see more of Ireland while we're at it."

"He's lying. He found my uncle and set up a meeting as a surprise." Lance grinned at me. "Not like I minded at all."

"Oh yeah, that sounds rough," the driver said as he pulled away from the airport. "What do you plan on doing while you're here?"

As we drove, the two of us watched as we made our way deeper into Dublin. "We want to see as much as we can. Anything you can suggest we don't miss?"

"If you do the bus tour, it takes you past everything in Dublin, and you can choose to either get off the bus and explore or just ride around the city. It's a great way to see a lot of things, fast."

"Oh yes, Lance mentioned that our hotel is close to one of the stops. We'll be here in Dublin for a few days, then we're renting a car to drive to Castlecomer, and we'll spend a few days touring the area."

I looked over and Lance was nodding off. We'd either need to get some caffeine, or go right to bed, and since it was still early, it was probably smarter to stay awake a while longer and get used to the time change. But I didn't have it in me to wake him. A few minutes later we pulled up to the hotel, and as soon as the car stopped moving, Lance woke up.

"It's okay, we're just at the hotel," I said, as he looked around, confused.

"I can't believe we're here," Lance said, and after grabbing our bags, stopped long enough to take in everything around us. It was a busy street, and I was sure we could keep ourselves occupied in this area for quite a while.

"Me either. Let's get checked in, and we can decide what we do next." After thanking the driver, the two of us stepped inside.

It was an older hotel, but it was clean and very nice. The person at the front desk seemed to understand we were exhausted and hurried to get us our room. Thankfully, we were on the first floor, so it wasn't much trouble to get there.

Lance flopped face down on the bed as soon as we were inside the room. "Oh my god, I don't think a bed ever felt so good," he mumbled.

"It's still pretty early. What do you think of going for a little walk and finding some food before we pass out?"

"If I can motivate myself to move, it sounds great." He made a half-hearted attempt before slumping back down onto the bed.

"Okay, enjoy your super-short nap. I'm going to splash some water on my face, brush my teeth, and hope for the best." I walked into the bathroom, and he had yet to move. Splashing water on my face definitely helped, but when my eyes met my own in the mirror, it was clear even to me how much *I* needed to sleep.

I walked out to the bedroom, and Lance was still where he'd landed on the bed. He lay there motionless as his breathing slowed in the throes of sleep. I didn't have it in me to wake him up, so instead I slipped my shoes off and lay down next to him. We could go out later if we still wanted to, but right now it was obvious we both needed sleep. Pulling him close, I nuzzled into his hair.

"I love you," I whispered into his ear. He took in a deep breath and let it out slowly as we relaxed into our first sleep in Ireland.

Five
Jet Lag

LANCE

"I'm awake," I yelled. But when I opened my eyes, the room was dark, and Billie was curled up next to me, asleep. That flight had been horrible, and I was glad we didn't have any schedule to keep and were able to adjust to the time difference at our own pace.

Billie mumbled something in his sleep before rolling over and settling again. I lay there for a while, just staring at the ceiling and thinking of all the things we planned to do while here. Finally, I took my phone out and scrolled through it killing some time. I fell asleep just as the sky was beginning to brighten.

"Good morning, sleepyhead," Billie whispered next to my ear.

I opened my eyes to find him just a few inches from me. "Good morning. We're in Ireland." I still couldn't believe it, but maybe it would finally feel real once we were out and running around.

"We are. It seems so incredible. I'm ready to explore Dublin. What do you think?" Billie asked.

"I think, hell yes. But first I need some caffeine, and possibly some food." I smelled my shirt, which happened to be the same shirt I wore on the plane. "And a shower, definitely a shower."

Billie rolled over the top of me and stood next to the bed with his hand out. "Care to join me in our first shower in Ireland?"

"Like I could say no to that." We both hurried to strip and piled into the bathroom. I turned the shower on and waited for it to get warm, but after a few minutes, it was still ice cold. "Let me try this." I pressed the big red button on the top of the faucet that I'd never seen on any faucet I'd ever used before, and the water was instantly hot. Then I noticed how deep the bathtub was, and how narrow.

"Do you think there's room for the two of us?" Billie asked as he peeked over my shoulder.

I turned to meet his eyes. "We'll make it work." And we did. It was a little tight, but we both liked being close, and I didn't mind him washing my back at all.

"I'm so ready for some food and a coffee," Billie said as we dressed.

"That's at the top of my agenda, too. Maybe we can look online while we're at breakfast and make a plan for the day."

"Yeah, we've got to stay awake and get used to the time," Billie said as he tugged a shirt on.

"I wanted to last night, but my body said nope."

Billie laughed at that. "Once your eyes shut, you were out."

"I barely remember leaving the airport. Remind me to save up for business class next time." The sleep I'd had on the plane was definitely not enough. The flight was long and the stress of the days leading up to our trip had taken its toll.

"I wouldn't mind business class, but I was very happy using your shoulder to nap on." He grinned at me and even if it bugged me, there was not a chance I'd ever complain. It felt good to have someone to share these experiences with, and the fact it was Billie made everything that much better.

After making sure we had what we'd need for the day, we stepped outside the hotel. The street was busy as everyone rushed to wherever they were off to. "Can I just say how nice it is to not feel like there's someplace we need to be?" I reached for Billie's hand, and he smiled at me before weaving our fingers together.

"It all looks so different from Stoney Brook," he said as we walked along a row of houses that all had basement entrances. Each door was a different color, and it just fit. It was both charming and clever at the same time. We'd walked about a block when we saw a small café. It was brimming with activity as people walked in and ordered their coffee or tea and breakfast. Neither of us needed to ask if this was where we should eat. We both just moved toward it.

A light drizzle had started, and as we hurried inside, I was thankful we'd both thought to wear a light jacket. It was warm, and the smell of coffee and baked goods all mingled together to make it even more inviting than it had looked from outside. Tall wooden shelves on the wall behind the counter and two glass cabinets held too many treats to try to choose just one. "I think I want one of everything," I said, just as a tall woman with short-cropped, black hair asked in a beautiful Irish accent what we'd like.

"I'll take a large coffee with extra cream, and can you just pick out two pastries for me? I can't choose."

"Sure thing. Can I get you something else?" She smiled and looked between the two of us.

"I'll have a large latte, and a breakfast sandwich," Billie said.

"Wait right here and I'll get it for ya." She turned, and after only a few minutes, she had it all on a tray and ready for us.

"Where do you want to sit?" Billie asked as he balanced the tray.

"The window." It was what he would choose and didn't need to turn to make sure he was behind me. I knew he would be. We sat down and Billie walked back to the counter to return the tray, I watched as he thanked the same woman and grinned as he walked back to his seat. I could watch him for the rest of my life, and it still wouldn't be enough.

"This is such a cool place." He sat down and we looked outside at the busy street. We were on Grafton Street and the area was blocked off from vehicle traffic, so only pedestrians were allowed. It was still early in the morning, but the street was a buzz of energy.

"So, what did you want to do first?" Billie asked and groaned as he took a sip of his coffee.

"Is it good?" I asked and blew on my own cup.

"It's only slightly less hot than lava, but it's delicious." He took a big bite of his sandwich made of thick cut bread toasted, with eggs and bacon. He waved his sandwich at my pastries. "Go on, try them and tell me how good they are."

One of them looked more like a candy bar with a cookie layer topped with caramel and a thick layer of chocolate. The other was a strawberry scone with a generous dollop of whipped cream on the plate next to a small jar of jam. I tore off a piece and drizzled some cream on it before popping it in my mouth. Now, I'd had many scones before, but none of them compared to this simple pastry. It was crisp on the outside but delicate and light on the inside. The cream was just sweet enough, and the pastry just salty enough, and mixed with the sweetness of the strawberries, it was perfect.

"You want to add those to the menu, don't you?" Billie said from across the table, the amused look on his face making me smile.

"They're so good. I'm not sure why, but they're so much better than any I've had at home. This would be such an excellent addition to the breakfast menu. Or even something special we could have in the late afternoon. Do you think they'd be willing to tell us how they make them?" Excitement flowed through me, and the jet lag that had dragged me down lifted.

"I think we're going to need to start a list of all the different things we want to add, and maybe take pictures of them," Billie suggested as he reached for the other pastry. After taking a bite, the look on his face told me he'd want to add this one too. "Just taste it. You'll understand."

I took the chocolaty treat from him and as soon as I tasted it, I knew he was right. "This would be so easy to sell. And it would package well to take in the truck if we wanted to do that. I love it." My mind raced with all the ways we could use just the two treats we'd tried, and if the rest of the trip went the same way, we'd return with a whole new menu. My thoughts went to the uncle I'd soon be meeting, and I realized I was even more excited now we were so close. "Billie, thank you for bringing me here." His eyes softened as he placed his hand over mine and stole the rest of the delicious chocolate, caramel, and shortbread treat. "Do you think that bread is fresh baked?" I asked, and Billie laughed. Only he could understand this obsession with food. It was one more reason I loved him so much.

Six

Dublin

BILLIE

Dublin was different from any place I'd ever been. The city was busy, but it had a small-town feel to it for reasons I couldn't begin to explain. Mingled in with the various businesses and pubs, there were many historical buildings that stood out to me like a beacon.

"What do you want to see first?" Lance asked as we strolled along a quiet street, away from the hustle and bustle.

"I want to see it all. Let's get on the bus and see everything there is to see, then decide what we want to see more of." I took out my phone and found the information to buy a bus ticket. It drove around the entire city, stopping at every tourist site, with a guide onboard to tell you exactly what you were looking at. Lance stood next to me, but his attention was on the surrounding city, and all the buildings that looked so different from both Sacramento and Maine.

"Okay, I have tickets for the double-decker bus we saw earlier. We just need to find the closest stop, which, if I'm reading this right, is just about a block away." He draped his arm over my shoulders and let me lead the way while looking at my phone for directions. When we were at the designated bus stop, we both stood to the side and waited, along with a few other people.

It wasn't long before a bright red bus pulled up in front of us. We boarded and climbed the narrow stairs to the top level. The tour guide sat near the front of the bus, welcoming everyone on board. He was a big man, with long red hair, a scruffy beard, and a newsboy hat. He looked like he'd be more comfortable sitting on a barstool in a pub rather than narrating a tour of the city.

"Welcome aboard, everyone. Now, you may notice all the pubs and colorful doors, well, Dublin is far more than what you see as we drive down the street," he said as he began his spiel.

The bus rumbled and swayed along as we drove past buildings packed so tight on a block there wasn't an inch of space between them, to historical buildings that were hundreds of years old. He warned us about which tourist traps to stay away from and told us to be sure to go to the Guinness factory for a free beer.

"This building is where Bram Stoker lived as an adult after graduating from Trinity College. In a few minutes we'll drive past Saint Anne's Church where he was married, and another interesting fact is he worked as a civil servant at Dublin Castle for a time," the tour guide said as we slowly made our way down the street.

"This is the natural history museum, which was started by Doctor Livingston."

"I knew we'd see a lot of history here but it's so incredible, it doesn't seem real," Lance said, not taking his eyes off the building to the side as we passed a small brown shop with *Burrito* painted in bright yellow letters.

Most of them were built of brick, which stood out to me being from California, where brick buildings were rare. A few buildings were completely covered with ivy and absolutely beautiful. One massive building made of a grey stone, fronted with huge pillars and appeared to have curved walls, came into view on the opposite side of the street.

"What you're looking at is the Bank of Ireland. You'll notice there are no windows; that's because all the light comes in from the roof. It's really quite amazing." The two of us looked at everything he pointed out, and we were both quiet as we waited to see what he'd point out next.

"The building you see here is from the twelfth century . . ."

That was all I heard before my mouth dropped open and I stared at a building that was far older than anything I'd seen before. Christ Church Cathedral was a blend of a castle and a medieval church with giant spire covered walkways and stained-glass windows. "I want to go into some of the cathedrals," I said as I tried to take in everything about it.

"We can go wherever you want." Lance smiled at me and seemed to get more enjoyment out of my excitement than all the wonders we were seeing. The light drizzle from earlier started again, and even though we both had jackets on, we decided to get off at the next stop. We made our way down the stairs just as the bus slowed and stopped.

"Would you like one?" the driver asked and held out two folded maps.

"Yes, thanks." I took them and handed one to Lance. We stepped onto the curb just as the drizzle turned to rain. "This way," I said, and grabbed Lance's hand before walking toward the enormous cathedral ahead. I had no idea what to expect inside, but it had to be drier in there than it was outside. We hurried to the entrance, passing green grass and a beautiful area where I imagined people gathered to enjoy a rare sunny day. Lance opened the door, and we were immediately overwhelmed by the sound of people as we entered St Patrick's Cathedral. The acoustics inside did little to dampen the noise of conversations and footfalls. But when we turned and looked at the full length of the ancient church, it took my breath away. High ceilings, crisscrossed with heavy beams

curved into several arches, ran the entire length of the building while on each side, large pillars divided the long room into
three sections.

"Whoa," Lance said, as the two of us tried to control our en-
thusiasm at seeing a building that was far older than America
itself. After paying an admission fee, we started to explore. A
plaque on the wall explained that this building had originally
been started in 1100 and told how it had changed through the
many years. It all seemed so fantastic and a little unreal.

"I can't wrap my mind around it being so old," I murmured,
as we started to move deeper into the building. It looked big
when we walked in, but after wandering around, it was far
more vast than I originally thought. From the ancient crypts to
the statues and crests honoring different people through the
ages. From royalty to clergy, so many had passed through this
place, and a few were interned underneath it, or maybe even
in the walls.

"Let's go see what's back there," Lance said, and we walked
toward the far end of the building.

"Look at the tile," I pointed out and stopped to give them
a better look. Some of them reminded me of Mexican tile
designs while many looked Gaelic, but they all combined to
make the floor just as amazing as every other surface. Large
stained-glass windows covered the rear wall, and I noticed
then, the grey stone walls were blackened. I wasn't sure if it
was from a fire or just age, but it all made it perfectly clear
this was an ancient building, and the fact it was still in such
incredible shape was something the makers would have been
proud of.

"Billie," Lance said, and turned to take both my hands.
"Thank you so much for bringing me here. I never in a million
years would have ever done this on my own, and in one day
you've shown me more than I would have ever dreamed of.
It's stunning here. Every little thing we've seen so far has been

unbelievably amazing and sharing it with you has made it that much better."

My eyes prickled with tears, and I wasn't sure if it was the fact I still needed more sleep, or that we were in an ancient cathedral surrounded by people from all over the world under a wall of stained glass. "I'm so glad we came," I managed to say. All that really mattered was the man in front of me and the way he looked at me. His eyes were full of light and love, and more emotions that all filled my heart with even more love for him.

Seven

A Tour

LANCE

Dublin was more than I could have ever dreamed of but seeing it through Billie's eyes made it even better. We walked outside the cathedral to find the rain had stopped and it was now a sunny day. "They weren't kidding when they said you can see all the seasons in Ireland in one day."

"Who said that?" Billie asked.

"I don't know, some guy on the bus," I said, and wrapped my arm around his shoulders. "He was cute, too. Blond hair and beautiful eyes." I nuzzled my nose into his hair and took a deep breath of the scent I'd know anywhere. It wasn't his shampoo or his soap, it was him.

"Should I be jealous?"

"No, baby, it's you," I whispered in his ear, making him shiver.

"Lance, if we're going to see more of Dublin—which I really want to do—then you gotta stop or I'll end up calling a ride to go back to the room." He ducked from under my arm and held me back by the tops of my arms.

"Would that be a bad thing?" I pouted my lip out and hoped he thought it was cute.

"No. It wouldn't be a bad thing, but I'd hate to miss the Guinness factory, or the library at Trinity University. You know, because Bram Stoker graduated from there."

"There is no way I'd live that down. Come on then. On to the next stop." We walked down the street to the stop the bus would pick us up from and this time we sat inside just in case it decided to rain again.

"We should get an umbrella. I think the locals know what they're doing, and most of them seem to have an umbrella," Billie said as he looked out the window. The bus pulled away from the curb and the tour began again.

The area we were driving through looked older than the last, and the tour guide explained that there were once many whiskey distilleries in this area. Now the narrow street lined with old brick buildings seemed to be all residential space above a variety of businesses. We passed by a building with a corner that was crumbling. I wasn't sure if it was left as an artistic look, or if it really was a part of the building that was starting to collapse. My thoughts were interrupted by a voice on the speaker.

"In 1875, a fire broke out at an old storehouse in this area. As it burned, the casks of whiskey being stored there exploded. They say the streets ran with whiskey that day, as many hurried to save what they could in their own pitchers and tankards," the tour guide said.

"There is nothing that would make me drink that, can you imagine?" Billie said.

"No. I'm not a huge whiskey fan to begin with. Add the fact it was flowing down the street along with who knows what. No thanks." My lips curled at the idea, especially knowing how hard we tried to keep everything sanitary in our businesses.

We turned a corner and were now in a more industrialized zone. Cranes were visible all across the area, standing high above the tallest building, and I wondered what they were working on. We passed under a black bridge with the Guinness label. "Should we go do the tour?" I asked and hoped Billie would say yes.

He rolled his eyes before answering. "How could I say no to you?" Biting his lip, he looked at me from under his eyelashes as the bus pulled to a stop just out front of the factory, and I wondered again why we were wasting our time on a bus tour when we could be back in the room. "I know what you're thinking. We'll have time for that later." He took my hand and pulled me along behind him until we were standing at the entrance of the Guinness Storehouse. Large brass letters spelled out the Guinness name, complete with their trademark harp.

We walked in and took the elevator that led to the tour. The building was immense, and when the elevator opened, it was to a large room with exposed pipes and old brick. Beautiful, and not at all what I expected. "Should we see how long the tour takes?" I asked, and we followed the signs in that direction.

There were so many people wandering around. It was hard to believe this was a brewery and that it was as old as it was. The smell of hops permeated the air, and I drew in a deep breath to appreciate it a little more.

"It says we have an hour before the tour starts," Billie said.

"We can go eat lunch. I saw a sign for a restaurant."

"Let's go," he said.

We followed a curved walkway that led right to what was made to look like a pub but was actually a small restaurant. After ordering, we found a seat near a window. "It does not feel like we're this high up." All of Dublin seemed to be laid out before us from here.

"I was thinking the same thing. I thought we were just a few floors up. This is a great view," I said, as the two of us were both fixated on everything beyond the window. The city was full of energy below us and one of the cranes we'd seen on the way in raised a load of metal into the air.

"What did you want to see next?" Billie asked.

"I thought you wanted to see the library?" I wasn't sure what exactly that was, but he'd been so excited to see it and if he wanted to see it, we would.

"Oh yes. We can stay on the bus until we get there if you're ready to call it a day."

"I don't want you to miss anything. If there's more you want to see, I want us to see it." I wasn't normally one to wander around and explore everything, but I knew Billie loved it. And I wasn't going to be the one that ruined a trip he'd taken so much care in planning.

He looked out the window a while longer before his eyes met mine. "I really want to see it." He clenched his teeth and shrugged his shoulders with an apologetic look.

"Then you're going to see it. That's what we're here for, right?"

"Well, mostly for you to meet your uncle." Billie grinned and played with the knuckle of my finger.

"I know there's not a chance I'd be here if it wasn't for you. And I know I've already said that, but it's true. Billie, you mean the world to me, and I still can't believe you went to so much trouble to plan a trip for me, for us. But I want you to see everything you've ever wanted to see while we're here. Even if it's the world's largest piece of cheese."

"I think that's somewhere in the US," he said.

"You're probably right." We both laughed and for a moment we enjoyed the view and the quiet murmur of the small restaurant, but when our meals arrived, that had our immediate attention. Stacked high with all the fixings and a freshly baked bun with the Guinness logo toasted on it, the burgers were definitely impressive. It was all held together with a wooden handled steak knife and surrounded by thick cut fries. Or chips, as they were called here.

"So, food, the tour, and then off to the university?" Billie asked as he readied his burger for a bite.

"That sounds like a perfect day to me." Any day we spent together was perfect, and even though I knew he was excited to see more, thoughts of what we'd do once we were back at the room were all I could think of.

"I know what you're thinking, and I promise as soon as we get back to the room—"

I cut him off with a raised brow, and what I hoped was a heated stare. He swallowed hard, took a drink of his beer, and nodded. "The things I'm gonna do to you," I whispered.

Billie had just taken a bite and for a second, I worried he'd choke before he took a drink and wiped his mouth. "Maybe we can skip the tour?"

Eight

Souvenirs

BILLIE

The day went by far too fast. We saw so much, and it made me hunger for more. Everything was amazing, and it seemed every corner we turned led to something else I wanted to explore.

"Babe, I have to admit, I wasn't excited to go to the university and see the library. I was imagining it being like any other library," Lance said as we walked back to the hotel.

"I knew it." I grabbed his hand and pulled him to my side. "What do you think now that you've seen it?"

"It's amazing. I had no idea what the book was they kept mentioning—"

"The Book of Kells."

"Yeah, that's it. I didn't know what it was. I'm still not completely sure I understand what it is, but it's beautiful. And old. So old."

"The look on your face when you were standing at the end of the long hall . . . it was all so much to take in. It's amazing and I never want to forget the feeling when we walked inside. I was a little surprised to see you buy some souvenirs." Lance was a very minimal person, and the fact he was bringing a part of Trinity College home with us said a lot to me.

The two of us took our time walking to the room. The hotel was older, but it was well maintained, and it was fun staying right downtown. We walked in and Lance immediately sat on the bed and took his treasures of the day out of the bag. He was like a kid, examining each one with a sweet smile on his face.

"Remember when we first met, and you were such a grouchy old guy?"

"No, I don't know what you're talking about," he said without meeting my eyes, and I knew he knew exactly what I was talking about.

"Okay then. Tomorrow, we'll pick up the rental car. Did you want to drive, or should I give it a try?"

Lance thought about it before answering. "I think you should drive, and I'll navigate," he said with a nod.

"Are you sure? I've never driven on the left before." I was really hoping he'd drive. I mean, he normally did, and I navigated, but if that's what he wanted, I was willing to try.

"I can if you want me to." He stuffed his treasures into his suitcase and walked back to where I sat on the bed.

"No, I want to try. If things go to shit, then you can take over."

His eyes widened and he plopped down next to me. "What do you mean? You're an excellent driver."

"Oh, you know, if I drive on the wrong side of the road, hit something, get us lost in the middle of nowhere, or—any of the above."

"Okay," he said, and gave me a look that left no doubt I would not be driving. "Don't worry, baby, I'll drive us around."

I tried not to show my relief, but I was relieved. Driving was something I enjoyed, but I'd driven on the right side of the road my whole life, and I wasn't so sure my brain wouldn't default back to that if I wasn't paying attention. "Okay, if you want to. I mean, I'm more than willing, but I don't mind letting you do it."

He grinned before pushing me back on the bed. "My jet lag is much better tonight." He breathed the words against my neck while the tip of his nose traced my jaw, and he ground down on me. I sucked in a deep breath before rolling him over and holding his hands above his head.

"So is mine," I whispered, and traced his ear with barely there touches of my tongue. He shivered and his hands tightened on mine. It was my turn to grind down on him, and I made sure he felt everything and more.

In a surprising move, he flipped me over and with a speed that startled me, he slid my jeans off and wasted no time in pulling my boxers down and flinging them over his shoulder. His complete focus was on me, and my hard dick that was close enough for me to feel his warm bursts of breath. I struggled not to grab his hair and pull him closer, but I wanted to see what he did next.

Without hesitating, he swallowed me down, making my back arch off the bed and shoving my dick deeper into his mouth. He grabbed my ass and buried his face in my groin, forcing a sound from me full of lust and need. "Jesus!" I finally managed to say.

He peered up at me while still swallowing me down deep. He loved this, the way he could make me come undone so easily, and his total control. I squirmed, fighting for control, and I hoped he knew I was close and would slow down while also wanting him to keep going. His mouth slid off me with a pop, and it was then I realized I still had my shirt on, and he was fully dressed.

He pulled me up with both hands, and slipped my shirt over my head, never taking his eyes off me, and not saying a word. He then positioned me facedown over the edge of the bed and trailed his hands down my back. "Don't keep me waiting any longer." The sounds of his pants on the floor and the click of the tube of lube made my hips move, involuntarily searching for friction.

"Patience," he whispered in my ear, knowing exactly what I wanted, needed, and felt. Slowly—so fucking slowly—he pressed into me as I clawed at the bed and tried to force myself not to press back against him. It was a game we played with each other. Driving us to the edge of passion and forcing the restraint I hoped was there, to hold us back.

"Fuuuuck." I drew the word out as Lance held himself deep inside me until I thought I'd lose my mind. Without warning, he pounded into me. The bed moved and creaked as I clung to it, and hoped it was as solid as it seemed, and we wouldn't end up paying for it on check-out.

Lance continued to pound into me until I was sure I'd lose my mind, or the bed would end up in a pile of rubble. His rhythm faltered, and I knew he was close. I tried to tug my hand away from where he still held mine above my head, but he resisted before finally his hand slid down my body. As soon as he gripped me, I had to fight for control, and that first stroke was both heaven and hell all in one.

"Not yet," he whispered, his voice full of sex and grit as he stroked me to the rhythm of his hips. Groans escaped my lips, but I wasn't coherent enough to worry we were being way too loud, and it was only mid-afternoon.

He gasped before pausing just long enough to put me over the edge. When I fell, I brought him with me, and it was intense, overwhelming, and immediately made me want more. We were both breathless as he rested across my back and planted gentle kisses on my shoulder. "I love you," he whispered. Even without him saying the words, I knew it was true. Every touch and motion showed me without him saying it.

"I love you too." I leaned back and kissed those sweet lips. "And you're totally driving."

Nine

Driving on the Left

LANCE

The next morning, we woke up a little more rested than the day before. I would never discount jet lag ever again. I rolled over to pull Billie close, but before I had a chance, he was up and rushing to the bathroom.

"Not today. I want to get going early, and I know if I stay in that bed, we won't be leaving for a while." He shut the door and after the toilet flushed, I heard him turn the water in the shower on.

I stood, and after stretching, I walked into the bathroom. "Mind if I join you?"

He opened the shower door and held his hand out. "Come on in, it'll take less time if we shower together. But no funny business," he said, and kissed my shoulder when I stood in front of him under the spray.

Billie wasn't kidding when he said he wanted to get going early. We were both dressed, had our bags packed, and were outside waiting for a car within an hour.

"I know, but it'll be worth it when we get to Castlecomer and you get to spend the afternoon with your uncle."

"I know you're right, but I was pretty happy in bed with my boyfriend." I reached for his free hand and squeezed it, and he instantly relaxed against my side.

"Keep that energy for the new hotel. I think it's a small place." Billie scrolled his phone looking for the hotel information, but before he found it a car pulled up in front of us.

"Mornin', boys, you waiting for a ride?" an older man asked from the front seat of a white sedan.

"Yes," Billie said, and the two of us hurried to put our bags in the back.

"Where are you headed today?" he asked as we slid into the back seat.

"The airport. We're picking up a rental car."

"Alright then," he said before pulling into traffic. Dublin was once again busy this morning. The streets we drove on were teeming with people walking and driving. The airport wasn't far, and as we drove in that direction, I realized I really was excited to drive around the countryside and meet an uncle I'd only recently learned about.

"What are you thinking?" Billie asked.

"I'm excited about what we'll see while we're driving."

"Where do you plan to go?" the driver asked, meeting my eyes in the mirror.

"We're going to Castlecomer. Lance has a relative there we're going to meet," Billie told him.

"It's a pleasant drive out that way. You'll enjoy it." He turned into the area of the airport where it seemed every rental car agency was located.

After thanking him and unloading our bags, we walked into the building. It was, of course, packed with people. Apparently, everyone needed a rental car at the exact same time we did. The company we'd booked with was located off to the right, so we both hurried through the crowd, and I hoped the line didn't grow any longer than it already was.

Billie walked up to the counter when our turn finally came, and he worked his magic. Within twenty minutes, we were walking out to the parking lot and choosing our car. There was a row of around ten similar cars, and we were told it didn't matter which one we chose, so Billie opened the trunk on a small black car made by a company I didn't recognize. The bags barely fit, but after a bit of shuffling around they were all stowed.

As soon as I closed the trunk, he tossed the key fob at me. "You're driving," he reminded me.

I slid into the seat and had to admit to myself how weird it felt to be sitting behind the wheel on the right instead of the left. Billie glanced at me and grinned while he buckled in. "Ready?" he asked.

"Yep, just trying to figure it all out before I actually start driving." I'd been driving since I was old enough to get my license, but this car had a manual transmission which meant shifting gears with my left hand instead of the right.

"I've mapped out where we're going, so just follow the directions on the phone. Easy peasy." Billie thankfully interrupted me overthinking everything, momentarily calming my nerves.

"Yeah, easy peasy," I mumbled before starting the car. It was a compact, which was probably a good thing, but it felt like it might not give us enough protection from whatever hazards I imagined could happen. I shook my head and tried to forget all that and just drive. We backed out of the space and exited the parking lot. "Okay, this isn't so bad." I followed the directions and came to a stop sign on what looked like an overpass. But it had a fucking roundabout on top.

"Oh shit," Billie said.

I sat there for a second and tried to figure out exactly how this worked and, after starting to turn right and realizing I needed to go straight, I veered to the left and entered the circle.

"It's two lanes," Billie said, his voice a little frantic as I crawled along at a speed barely above standing still.

"What do you mean?" There were no lanes marked, but I saw the sign he must have seen and realized that yes, I was driving in the middle of what was meant to be two lanes.

"Turn there," Billie pointed, and I noticed his hand was clutching the handle above the door.

Swerving to the left, I could now see it led onto a freeway, and I was relieved it was straight and wide, and not too heavily traveled. Then I glanced at the speedometer and noticed it was kilometers, not miles. "What's the speed limit?" I asked and looked around, hoping for a sign.

"Oh uhm, doesn't matter, there's the turnoff," Billie said, and pointed to a sign that read Castlecomer.

I swerved in the direction of the exit and tried to adjust to going from a wide-open freeway to a narrow country lane.

"You're really close over here," Billie said, and I realized I was driving so close to the shoulder the plants on the side of the road were brushing along his side of the car. I adjusted to the right, but then a tractor—a fucking tractor—was approaching in the opposite direction and I might have said a silent prayer that we didn't side-swipe it as we passed.

"Holy shit, that was close," Billie said. But he didn't need to tell me. We continued on for a few miles, or kilometers. Whatever the fuck it was, my mind was racing, trying to keep track of the lane we were in, the gearshift being on the left, and the speed that I still wasn't sure of. I took a left turn that led to a narrow bridge. The whole car bounced, and I forced myself not to look at Billie, as I was pretty sure I'd hit the curb. Thank god Billie had insisted on the full coverage insurance.

"It's beautiful," Billie said, and I relaxed enough to look around and enjoy the landscape. A windmill slowly turned on the side of a hill that was a green I'd never seen before. We passed by small paddocks and fields separated by stone fences and rolling hills, and heavy wooded areas all in a short distance.

Finally, feeling a little more confident, I reached across and rested my hand on his leg. "It is beautiful, and I still can't believe we're here."

"Me either, but I'm so glad we're here together. Even if you did plow through those plants on the side of the road and hit the bridge back there."

I glanced at him, and when I did, he barked out a laugh. "Oh my god, I thought I was going to kill us," I admitted and joined him in laughing.

"You're doing great," he said, and rested his hand on mine. "And there's no way in hell you're talking me into driving."

Ten

Lunch

Billie

I tried not to show it, but I had serious doubts we'd make it there without a dent or possibly losing a bumper. We were so close to that stone wall I could make out the small bits of stone in the mortar.

"This is weird," Lance mumbled as he followed the navigation. It had us turn off the road we were on and take a much narrower road that seemed to go into the small town we were near rather than around it.

"Are you sure this is the right way?" I asked, knowing he had no clue.

He glanced at me with his classic *what the fuck* look he usually reserved for customers that stepped on his last nerve and looked a few times between the navigation and the road we were on. Cars were parked along both sides of the road, narrowing the already narrow road down to a single lane.

"Oh, fuck, this is too narrow." His hands tightened on the wheel as he tried to correct and not hit any of them. The distinct thunk on my side let us both know he'd gotten too close. I rolled the window down and flipped the mirror back into place.

"Guess you were right," I said and tried not to smile.

"Oh my god, if it gets any narrower, I'm pulling over and we're calling for a ride." He looked in the rearview mirror. "Keep an eye out for cops."

I wanted to laugh, but I knew his nerves were frazzled. About a mile down the road, it opened up a little. The houses and buildings were very close to the edge of the road, but the road was wide enough we weren't in danger of hitting an oncoming car, or a rock sticking out on the other side. Finally, a sign caught my attention.

"Turn in there." I pointed to the bright white building next to a small coffee place. The sign said it was a pub and restaurant, and since we had yet to eat, this sounded perfect. "Let's go get some food. Maybe no coffee for you."

"Oh, I think I need lots of coffee. It'll either wake me up or put me over the top." We both got out of the little car and stretched.

"We're in Ireland," I said, and grinned over the top of the car at Lance. He walked around the car and picked me up with a hug.

"Oh, did it do any damage when we hit?" he asked and set me on the ground to look.

I couldn't see anything, but I didn't really want to look that close. Lance brushed the mirror off one more time before taking my hand and leading me to the door of the pub.

The interior was painted in dark colors and accented with dark wood. After finding a staff member, they told us to go to the bar to order. We were the only ones there as we stood in a room painted a beautiful deep blue and decorated with antique silver trays adorning the walls. The bar was massive, and I imagined on a weekend it was not as quiet as we now found it.

"Have a seat where you want. I'll be right with you," an older man said as he walked in from another room. He handed us menus and walked behind the bar to get each of us a glass of water.

"Everything looks good," Lance said as we both looked over the simple menu. I was tempted to try the pizza but chose meat pie instead. Lance chose a pasta dish.

"How much longer until we get to the hotel?" Lance asked. I mapped it out on my phone to know for sure.

"It says it's thirty minutes, but if a tractor gets in the way, it might take longer." The barman brought our food out just then and grinned at me.

"Have a run in with one of the locals, did ya?"

"No, we just met it on the road. I was worried there wasn't enough room for the two of us."

"They can be a hazard, it's true." He set our food down, and I would have sworn I heard him laugh as he walked away.

"What do you want to do once we get there?" I took a bite of my pie, and this one was even better than the one I'd had in Dublin.

"I'm not sure. It might take me a minute to calm my nerves if the drive is the same as it was here." He widened his eyes before taking a big bite of his pasta.

"How about if we settle into the hotel, and if there's anything nearby, maybe we can explore? Your uncle's place is just across the street, and he's expecting us later today."

"Yes, I was thinking about that earlier. Do you think he really minds if we stop by? I know we planned to, but I don't want to seem too pushy."

"Lance, it's all planned. Don't worry, he wants to meet you as much as you want to meet him. And don't forget you brought the sourdough starter to share with him. You don't want that to go bad."

He dragged his hand down his face the way he did when we were halfway through a shift in the food truck, and he knew we were going to run out of food. "I've been questioning if that's a good idea or not. What if he thinks it's stupid?"

I stopped eating and rested my hand over the top of his on the table. "Lance, don't you dare doubt yourself. I know how much that starter means to you, and I think anyone who has ever made bread would appreciate it for what it is. You're sharing a piece of something you worked really hard on."

"I guess I just really want it to go well. I've never met a relative I had no clue I even had."

"Just be your usual charming self and everything will be great," I said, with a squeeze of his hand.

"You know you're talking to me, right? The one that hides by the grill to avoid peopling?"

I brushed off his comments with a kiss to his hand and stole a taste of his pasta. After we finished eating and ordering two coffees to go, we were back on the road. This time, the road was narrow, but there wasn't a stone wall running three feet away from the road. And about thirty minutes later, we crossed a narrow bridge and entered the little town of Castlecomer. Our hotel was just off the bridge, so we pulled into the parking lot and took in our smaller bags since we only planned to stay one night here.

We both stood for a moment and looked around. "This place is part of your family's history." His roots were here, whether he could feel it or not. This was where his family had originally come from.

"I suppose, in a way, I'm coming home." His face lit up as he took in the row of businesses across from the hotel, the small market next door, and the rest of the tree-lined street. The hotel was covered in ivy, and when we walked in, it was immediately clear it had once been a residence. This small town in Ireland held a part of Lance he hadn't even known about until recently, and now he'd get a chance to find out more.

Eleven

Sourdough

LANCE

After barely surviving the drive here, I was exhausted, and had serious second thoughts that it should be me driving. "I don't think I've ever been so happy to pull into a parking space," I said as I flopped on the bed. The room was nice, and the bed was comfortable. That's all that mattered to me.

"I'm so glad we got full coverage. Hopefully, the road to-morrow isn't as narrow."

"I'm relieved you not only suggested it but insisted on it. It's not something I normally get."

Billie walked into the bathroom before walking back out and grabbing something from his bag. "We should contact your uncle. He'll be expecting us soon."

"Should we call him or just go to his restaurant?" I wasn't sure how any of this worked. I couldn't wait to meet him, but I was also nervous about it. What if we had nothing to talk about? Or worse, we hated each other on sight?

"Lance, I know you're second-guessing this, but don't. I spoke to Joseph in a few emails, and he seems very nice. Like I said before, he's just as anxious to meet you as you are to meet him."

"Let's go see if we can find his business. This town is so small it shouldn't be too hard." I was going to get the jar of sourdough starter but paused, still not sure it was a good idea.

"Lance, you brought that starter all this way. Are you sure you don't want to share it?" Billie asked, and damn him for knowing me so well. I went to my suitcase and dug out the jar I'd taken so much care in packing and turned to face Billie.

"You're right, I'm taking it. He doesn't have to keep it if he's not interested. But what baker wouldn't be interested in this fabulous sourdough starter?" I tried to sound lighthearted about it, but the truth was, it meant more than I was willing to admit. We'd both had a part in the final product, and I liked knowing it was made with love.

The look Billie gave me said he knew exactly what I was thinking without him saying a word. "Let's go then. We can decide later if we want to see more of the town or not."

We took the elevator downstairs and walked right out onto the main street. A narrow path to the left followed the road and led across the bridge we'd driven over. To the right of the hotel was a row of small businesses. "Is his restaurant that way?"

"Yes, that's it there." Billie pointed, and the two of us crossed the street. One small restaurant was closed with the sign reading they were only open for breakfast. But the one at the end was open. It was small, and from the window I could see there was a single bakery display case on one side and a seating area of four tables just inside. The counter also served as a bar where stools were pulled up and seating was encouraged.

Before I could think about it, I opened the door and walked in. Two of the tables were full, while the rest of the place was empty. I wandered over to the bakery case and noticed the baskets of bread and rolls to the side.

"Afternoon. Can I help you?" a tall thin man with thick grey hair that stood up all over the place asked me, as he walked out from the back wiping his hands on his white apron.

"Yes, we're looking for Joseph Moran," Billie said with a smile.

"Well then, you've found him. What can I do for you?" His accent was strong, and for a minute, I wished I had that same accent. He looked between the two of us before rolling his eyes when neither of us answered.

"Sorry, I'm Billie and this is Lance, Lance—"

"Karl," Joseph finished for him with a snap of his fingers. "I see you finally made it back to the motherland." He grinned and crossed his arms before stepping up and hugging me. "It's good to meet you."

"It's good to meet you too," I said, still feeling overwhelmed.

"How was your drive out here?"

"Oh my god, it's a miracle we made it here in one piece." Billie laughed, and Joseph joined him.

"Have a seat, and I'll be right out. I just need to tell Nell that I'll be taking a break."

"Oh, I don't want to take you away from your business. We can come back at another time that's better for you," I offered, and I could tell Billie was asking me what the fuck I was doing without even looking at him.

"Your guy there said you'd try that. Sit down, I'll only be a minute." He hurried off, and Billie pulled out a chair at the closest table.

"We're not leaving until you get to talk to him," Billie said, and picked up one of the menus from the table.

I took a seat next to him and looked over at the menu he held in his hand. "Everything looks good, and what a variety. Salad bowls, toasted ciabatta sandwiches, seafood chowder, and desserts."

"Lance, does anything look familiar to you?" Billie asked, and I looked over the menu again. "What do you—oh my god, this is so similar to our menu. How did I miss that?"

"It's almost exactly the same except for the Irish breakfast. Maybe that's something we could add. And it looks like he could use a good lobster roll. Is that a thing here?" He was engrossed in reading the menu when Joseph returned.

"Sorry about that, so what do you think of Ireland so far?" he asked as he set a carafe of coffee on the table and poured us each a cup.

"We like it. Yesterday we rode the big red bus all around Dublin," Billie said.

"We got off at nearly every stop and walked a few miles. But it was all amazing. There's nothing like this back in the States." I glanced at Joseph to find him staring at me.

"Sorry, I don't mean to be rude. But you look so much like my father when he was a young man." He continued to look at my features until shaking his head and looking away.

Billie looked between the two of us. "Do you have a picture?"

"Not on me, but I could email you one. He was a baker by trade, and most of the recipes I use are his. He taught me when I was just a wee lad."

"My mom owns a restaurant that was started by our ancestors who migrated there from Ireland. They met on the voyage and were married soon after they arrived. He was the keeper of the lighthouse. My family still has a restaurant there."

"My father used to tell me that story, and his father told him. We're the same, you and me. The restaurant business is in our blood." His eyes crinkled as he grinned and I studied his face the way he'd studied mine, looking for familiarity.

"I suppose it is. Same as Billie. His family has been in the restaurant business for years." I squeezed his hand on top of the table and noticed Joseph's eyes followed the movement. "Billie and I have been together a few years now. We'll be engaged and married before too long." Billie's eyes met mine, making me grin like a fool.

"Oh, you two have it bad," Joseph said, and slapped me on the back. "I'll be expecting a wedding invitation when you set a date."

"Of course, you're invited," Billie said.

"I brought you something from the States. I wanted to share a sourdough starter from the bread I use in the restaurant. It took me forever to get it just right, and I thought you might like to try it."

He picked up the jar and slowly turned it. "How long did it take you to perfect it? I've tried a few sourdough starts and none have been quite what I want."

"When he said forever, he's not kidding. He worked on it every week for a few months. He even compared it to the one my family uses. His is a little less sour, but just as crusty," Billie said.

"Well then, what are you waiting for? Come on, let's give it a try." He stood and we followed suit, not sure exactly what we were doing. "Off to the kitchen, boys. I want to see how you make yours."

It was like music to my ears, and even if the kitchen was tiny, it had everything we needed, and soon the three of us were elbow deep in flour and bread dough, making sourdough in Ireland.

Twelve

Shepherd's Pie

Billie

We stayed at Joseph's café for the rest of the day. He locked the door and he and Lance talked about the intricacies of baking the perfect bread, and planning out how much to bake so you didn't have any wasted loaves.

"You two getting hungry?" Joseph asked.

"I can eat," Lance said, and patted his flat stomach.

"He can always eat," I said, making Joseph laugh.

"Must be a family thing," he said, and walked out of the bakery area and into the main kitchen, urging us to follow behind him. It was a very small space, not much bigger than the food truck. Joseph moved around, taking a few items out of a small refrigerator before picking out a variety of vegetables.

Without a word he got busy putting some potatoes on to boil and then chopping and mixing while Lance and I stood and watched. Next, he took out a saute pan and added some ground meat. Once it was browned, he added onions, and finally all the vegetables.

"What are you making?" Lance asked.

"My mum's shepherd's pie. We have a recipe we use here on special occasions, but this is our family recipe. I want to give it to you to carry on the tradition in our family. I know you could find something similar online, but it wouldn't be one you're connected to. This recipe is a part of you. Just like your bread is connected to our family, and now Billie's, too."

Lance's eyes got a little shiny, and he reached for Joseph's shoulder and gave it a good squeeze. Joseph turned to him and wrapped him in his arms in a big hug with a slap on the back.

"We're also huggers. You'll need to know that at some point." Joseph laughed and got back to cooking. "Now I know you're probably thinking this isn't a new recipe. But if you went into every house in Ireland, you'd find a different version in each one. Most passed down from generation to generation and shared along the way. The way I'm making it now is not the original, but I'll give you both recipes, so you can do with it what you want."

"Thanks, Joseph. I'm excited to try it," Lance said, while watching everything Joseph did.

"So how long are you staying?" Joseph asked.

"We're only here a week. I'm already trying to think of excuses to stay longer, but I know the restaurant will be a mess when we get back, and honestly, I don't like being away very long," Lance explained.

"He's lying. He's never taken more than a few days off. Lance is a very dedicated worker."

"Owner," Lance corrected.

"Co-owner."

"Co-owner," he agreed, and kissed my cheek.

"How does it work for you working together? The wife and I tried it and only lasted a few days. We're both a little opinionated," Joseph said, and grinned.

"Well, we met when he needed help at his food truck. From across the parking lot, I could see he was the only one working the truck at a big food festival. After sampling his signature lobster roll and going back for another, I offered to help, and he accepted."

"Billie's a hard worker. I admire that. And like he knew exactly what I needed, he just came in and took over. I never had to train him or tell him how to do anything, he just knew." His eyes held so much affection, and I was reminded how easy it was to fall in love with him, and how much I wanted to spend the rest of my life by his side.

"He tried to tell me what to do, but with the food truck, it was easy enough to go outside, send him orders, and let him do what he does best, cook. He knew I was doing a good job in no time, but mostly, he trusted me. I knew how much his business meant to him. That was obvious, but it meant a lot to me to know he trusted me immediately." We stood staring at each other for a moment until Joseph cleared his throat and took the potatoes off the heat.

"You two." He shook his head while he grinned a mile wide and moved to the sink and poured the boiling water off them.

"We hear that a lot," I said, and Lance laughed.

"So, what are your plans for tomorrow?"

"I want to see a castle, so we'll be stopping wherever the nearest one is," I said.

"Kilkenny Castle is quite a sight. It's been restored, and it is probably closer to what you expect a castle to look like. It's not far from here. There are a lot of ruins that you might find interesting along the way, and well, all around here, really."

"We passed a tall tower on the way. It almost looked like a smokestack, but I googled, and it said it's a tower." Lance's eyes shot to me, and he tipped his head in thought.

"I don't remember seeing that. Was it before we stopped to eat?" he asked.

"Yeah, a little before. It was after you hit the bridge and nearly took off the mirror. I thought you had enough going on, and since we're going back to Dublin, we can always find it again." I smiled at him before Joseph started laughing.

"Sounds like you two really had an adventure driving out here. Don't worry though, you can get on the N78 from here to Kilkenny and stick to the bigger motorways. Those narrow roads are a bit of an adjustment if you're not accustomed to them."

"Oh, it was an adventure alright." I didn't even look at Lance when I said it. I knew he was still a little on edge. We both watched as Joseph finished the filling before mixing and adding the mashed potatoes to the top of the dish.

"I noticed you added cheese to your potatoes. Is that how it's normally done?" I asked. I hadn't had shepherd's pie many times, so I wasn't sure what was expected and what was a family tradition.

"No, that bit's my Da's influence. He'd put cheese on a rock if he could chew it. He always said anything with cheese can't be all bad."

"I'd agree with that," Lance said.

"He's a big fan of cheese," I said.

Joseph slid the pan into the heated oven and wiped his hands on his apron as he turned to us. "Okay then, how about if I help you map out some places to go to around here that I think you'd find interesting?"

"That would be amazing," Lance said. "But just one request. If you can try to plan it around the bigger highways, I'd really appreciate it. I'm not sure my nerves could take another day like today, and even though we got full coverage insurance on the rental, I don't want to test it."

Joseph stared at him for a full minute before laughing loudly and slapping Lance on the back. "I'll do my best."

"Thank you so much. Seriously. Thank you," I added, and secretly hoped he didn't put us on any of the minor roads that crisscrossed the map of Ireland. "Anything wider than a bike path would be appreciated."

"I'll keep that in mind," Joseph said, and laughed again.

A while later we sat at a table in the small café. Joseph had called his family over to eat with us, and to meet the distant nephew he'd never heard of until recently. And the smile on

Lance's face told me bringing him here was exactly what he'd needed.

Thirteen
A Little More Time

LANCE

Sitting at the table in the small café in Castlecomer with Joseph's family—my family—was surreal. Mom had always talked about the family we had in Ireland, but I'd never met any of them, and now I was questioning why that was. They were a lovely bunch. A little loud, and very boisterous, but it was such a fun evening. And the fact Billie was there with me the whole time, and they included him the same as they included me, meant the world to me.

"Joseph, seys ye drive a truck with an enormous lobster on top of et," an older woman who sat opposite me said to Billie.

"Yes, it's his food truck. He specializes in lobster rolls when we go to festivals."

"Ye don't say. I think I'd quite like to see that," she said with a grin. Billie took out his phone and showed her a picture. She clapped her hands and laughed. "Oh my, ye weren't kidding. It is massive."

We all laughed, and I could see in her a family resemblance to my mother.

"What is it, Lance?" Joseph asked, and I realized I'd been staring at her.

"You just remind me of my mother," I replied, looking again at the older woman

"She does," Billie agreed and squeezed my hand on top of the table.

She was tiny, like my mom, and definitely had the same personality.

"Does she run her restaurant with military precision?" Joseph asked, his Irish accent coming on strong.

"Oh yes, she's tiny, but no one messes with her. She's a force to be reckoned with." She really was, and without her, this trip wouldn't have been possible. There wasn't another person I'd trust with my restaurant.

"Sounds like I need to get to know my American cousin a bit better. Oh, and since Joseph has no manners at all, my name is Fia. I know of your mother, but I'm not entirely sure we've spoken."

"She did say she'd met with some of her relatives here, but it was years ago." It was so easy to speak to them all, and I hated we only had tonight, but I was thankful we were able to spend time with them like this. Like a big old family.

Billie squeezed my hand and smiled, and I really believed he knew exactly what I was thinking.

We stayed late into the night, and when we finally walked back to our hotel, I realized we'd barely been there at all. But it was perfect with how close Joseph's café was. "Billie, I want you to know how much I appreciate you pushing me to meet Joseph. I know I wasn't all that excited about it. But I cannot imagine missing out on this. Thank you."

He leaned in close and kissed my cheek. "You're welcome, and don't worry, I'm sure Joseph would love to see you in the morning for breakfast before we leave."

"I can't believe he cooked for us all after we made sourdough. And they all liked it."

"Of course, they liked it. It's the best sourdough in Maine."

"You're the best, Billie, and I love you so much. Sometimes I can't believe how full my heart feels."

"Well, it's a good thing I love you just as much."

We walked into the hotel, and it was much quieter than it had been earlier. A couple sat in the corner of the lobby, close enough to the fireplace to enjoy the warmth but far enough away from everyone for privacy.

We walked into our room and both of us were quiet as we stripped and slid into bed. "I love you," Billie whispered.

"I love you too." I drifted off to sleep, content in the fact I had a new family that was warm and welcoming, and I couldn't wait to see again, and a boyfriend lying next to me that was the most precious man I'd ever met. Later, I dreamt of him walking up to the food truck that day, and thanked whoever I could that it was my truck he chose.

I was up early and showered before Billie was even awake, then when he still didn't wake up, I resorted to shaking the bed. "Wakey wakey, Billie," I whispered. He ignored me for a full minute before cracking an eye open.

"Why are you awake and so cheery before coffee?"

"I want to go to Joseph's again before we leave. I thought we could spend the morning there."

"So, I guess you didn't get enough of your Irish family last night?"

"I guess I didn't. Now hurry up, I want to try a traditional Irish breakfast," I said, quoting from the menu.

"Okay, give me a few minutes and we can go." With that, Billie was up, and in the bathroom, while I took the time to pack my bag. We'd be staying somewhere else tomorrow night, so might as well take the bags down when we went.

Billie kissed my cheek as he brushed past me and dropped his towel. "Are you trying to tempt me?" I asked, the luggage forgotten for now.

"Is it working?" Billie purred.

I walked over to where he stood looking as absolutely gorgeous as the first day we met and put my hands on his hips. "Oh, it's working." I kissed along his jaw and was lost in the warmth of him and the feel of his naked skin against me. Unable to resist, I wrapped my arms around him and kissed him. My tongue sought out his as we kissed like we hadn't seen each other in months.

He pulled back and panted while his forehead rested against mine. "Are you sure you want to go to breakfast?" he asked.

I smiled and lifted his chin for another kiss. "We can skip it if you'd like."

He pulled back enough to meet my eyes. "Lance, we flew halfway across the globe to meet your uncle. Who I think is awesome, by the way. If you want to go have breakfast with Joseph before we leave, we should probably go now, but you are totally making this up to me later," Billie said. "It was just getting good." He pouted.

I nibbled his bottom lip and caressed his jaw. "I am so making it up to you. Now come on, let's go try some haggis."

Billie slipped on a pair of boxers and turned to face me. "I draw the line at haggis, and black pudding. Sorry, but you're on your own there." Within twenty minutes, he was dressed, and we were walking to the car to put our luggage away.

"I'm so glad you're having fun," he whispered as he snuggled into my side after we'd tucked it all away in the trunk.

"I'm having the best time ever." I pulled him into a side hug and we both laughed and made our way back to the small café, that in one day felt familiar to me, welcoming, and very much like family. "Later, we can go to the big castle. I'm excited about that, and more than happy to know the road there isn't as narrow as the road here was."

"It's all an adventure," Billie said, in his worst and best Irish accent. We hurried across the street, and I stood for a moment and took in the small cafe.

"I want to remember every detail of our visit, and I want to keep in touch with Joseph." Billie nodded. He understood, just like he always did, and when we walked inside Joseph hugged him in a greeting as heartily as he hugged me.

"Now, which one of you is going to help me cook this morning?" Joseph asked.

He didn't need to ask me twice. I was more than ready to cook in the tiny kitchen that now seemed so familiar.

Fourteen

A Castle

BILLIE

Lance didn't want to leave. It was easy to see in the way he kept his eye on Joseph and watched every move he made. He'd helped Joseph in the kitchen until he'd chased him out and ordered him to have a seat and relax. Joseph brought us our breakfast and hurried off to help other customers while stopping to chat any chance he got.

"You know, we can stay longer if you'd like." I had to offer it. Finding his roots was the main reason for this trip, and even though we both loved everything we'd seen in Ireland so far, there was no way I wasn't going to give Lance every moment he could get with his family.

"No, I couldn't do that. I want you to see everything you wanted to see here, and not just this little café," Lance said, and took my hand.

"Let me see if the hotel is available for the rest of the week. We'll go see a few things during the day, then stay here and spend time with Joseph in the evening if he's available. What do you think?" His smile told me everything, and his kiss sealed it.

"If you're sure, I'd love to do that. Have I told you how much I love you?" He grinned at me, and if I hadn't heard his words, his expression would have told me he wanted this as badly as I knew he did. "I've had so much fun, and I feel like a hole has been filled with relatives I never knew existed."

"Plus, you need to make your lobster rolls for them," I said, and didn't need to explain to him who I meant because they were on his mind as we sat there.

"How difficult do you think it is to get lobster here?" Lance asked and immediately started searching on his phone for answers.

"I'm sure we can find it. It might be more expensive than we're used to, but you only get to share meals with your family so many times."

"Especially when they live so far from us," Lance mumbled.

"Don't worry about that now. Focus on what you want to do with them while we're here. Now, I really would like to see the castle Joseph recommended today."

"You'll be going to Kilkenny then?" Joseph asked as he stopped at our table with a tub full of dirty dishes after clearing off a table.

"Yes, I really want to see it. I looked it up, and I can't wait to see it in person." I squeezed Lance's hand, waiting for him to tell Joseph our plans.

"We're going to see if the hotel is available for the rest of the week. I'd like to spend more time with you and your family, Joseph. Opportunities like this don't come along all that often, and I don't want to waste it."

"Lance, you know you and your guy are welcome here anytime. And if you're staying longer, then I'm sure I can put you to work here." He laughed at that before picking up the tub of dishes. "But honestly, I'd love for you both to stay longer."

"Then we will. We'll go visit the castle and whatever else is around that area. When we get back, we'll see what you have going on. I'd love to cook for you one night, if you don't mind." Lance was so happy. He was not a man who was known to show much emotion, and maybe it was because we were so far from home, or maybe it was the fact he'd met relatives he already loved. But whatever the reason, I was glad to see him enjoying himself.

"I'd quite like for someone else to cook for me. Even if it is something from the States," Joseph said with a wide grin.

Lance shook a finger in his direction. "You'll eat those words. I just need to find a good source for seafood."

"I can help you there. I don't have much use for seafood, but I do have a supplier who can get it."

"How fast do you think they can deliver?" Lance asked, and I finished my breakfast and helped clear the table while he talked to Joseph. "Okay, now that you've worked it all out, can we go see the castle?"

"Yeah, and we can book the room through the hotel website," Lance said, and pulled me to the door. "Bye, Joseph, we'll see you later."

"We didn't need to rush off," I said as we crossed the street and walked back to the hotel.

"I know, but I want to see the castle too," he said, and kissed me on the cheek. "Check the hotel on the phone so we don't have to worry about it when we get back."

I took out my phone while we walked to the car and by the time we were driving away, I'd booked us through to the end of the week. "We're close to so many things. We can just go out each day and come back here when we've seen enough."

"Billie, do you think you'll *ever* see enough?" He tried not to smile but failed, so I punched him in the arm, just because I could.

"Probably not. Now come on, I want to see this castle." We drove along a road that, as Joseph promised, wasn't nearly as narrow as the one we'd driven here on. "I don't think I'll ever get used to how beautiful it is here." Everything was green, and the small paddocks marked out in stone fences along the way reminded me how different it was here from Sacramento or Maine.

When we pulled into the town of Kilkenny, we wove through neighborhoods and business districts until we were on the same street as the castle. It was massive, and in such good condition it made it hard to believe it was several centuries old. People walked along the wide sidewalk and up to the massive arched entrance.

"There's a parking space right out front," Lance said, and pulled in. We sat across the street, and I tried to imagine what this looked like before the modern streets and cars were here. "Let's go. I can't wait to see what it's like behind the entrance."

We paid our entry fee and walked through the entryway under a heavy wooden door and were immediately in a large courtyard. The castle was shaped like a U, with the entry being directly across from another wing. Out to the right was an endless expanse of green grass, and I imagined knights and commoners riding or walking up to the castle to speak to the members of the wealthy family that once ruled here.

We started the self-guided tour and the very first room we walked into was breathtaking. There were high ceilings, massive portraits, and windows along the length of the wall. The walls were painted a sage green with accents of red and gold, highlighted by several crystal chandeliers and a box-beamed ceiling painted white and outlined in gold trim. The floor was black and white tile covered with multiple large tapestry rugs, and multiple doors and doorways of heavy dark wood.

At one end of the room, antlers were mounted over a fireplace, but they were like nothing I'd ever seen. They had to be at least ten feet wide and were a tangle of different shapes and sizes of horn.

"That's an Irish Elk," a woman dressed in a skirt and wearing a vest with a name tag on it, said.

"Are they still around?" Lance asked.

"Oh no, they're an ancient species. Gone extinct long ago, I'm afraid."

We continued from room to room, being led by the map that we were handed when we walked in. There were so many rooms I had a hard time keeping track of what we'd seen and what was still ahead. Not only was the property a vast expanse of land, but so was the castle. Most of it had been refurbished to a close reconstruction of how it had when the wealthy owners had lived here.

I stood at a window looking out over the land when muscular arms wrapped around my waist and warm lips kissed my neck. "This is amazing," he whispered.

"Yeah? I wasn't sure how much you would actually like going to all this old stuff."

"I love anything that includes time with you."

He was happy. Happier than I'd probably ever seen him, and I was thrilled to be here to share it with him.

Fifteen

Plans

LANCE

We wandered around the castle, the first I'd ever seen from the inside, and the look on Billie's face made it all worth it. Driving on the narrow roads, the jet lag that I didn't want to complain about but still couldn't shake, and the forced time off that I now relished. "Mind if we check out the kitchen?" I asked, and Billie kissed my cheek.

"Not at all. I'm curious how they could make enough food for large parties here. I mean, they didn't have refrigeration, or a way to store things for long." He looked at the map of the property and we took a set of stairs that looked like it was going in that direction.

"I think I've walked more stairs since we've been here than I have in years," I said, as we both hurried down to the bottom floor. We turned a corner and stepped into an area that had been converted into what they called the tearooms. There were round cafe tables and a display of desserts, all of which looked tempting. We walked through that room and into what had been the original kitchen. Taking up most of one wall was a fireplace large enough to walk into, along with lots of long tables and counters probably used for preparation areas.

"Can you imagine cooking a big feast here?" I asked Billie.

"No, I can't. First, I don't know anything about cooking on an open fire like that, and second, they ate lots of wild game. I don't have experience with it either and I don't want to imagine having to pluck every chicken before you could cook it." He wrinkled his nose as he walked around and looked at every little kitchen gadget on display.

"Yeah, it's definitely different from what we're used to." We walked back into the tearoom and this time the smell of the delectable desserts got the best of me. "Let's have a snack before we go."

"I thought you'd never ask," Billie said. The two of us picked out the most decadent looking desserts we'd seen yet. "This is so cool. I can't believe how beautiful everything is."

"And big. Everything is big, beautiful, and old, so very old." I laughed as I took a bite of the chocolate dessert I'd chosen.

"So old," Billie agreed, and took a bite of his own dessert. "Oh, this is so good. We need to start collecting dessert recipes while we're here."

An hour later we were back on the road and driving around Kilkenny looking at the sights. "I can't get over how different it all is," Billie said as he looked out the window at all the houses and business we passed by.

"I think I could get used to it," I murmured.

"Do you? I hadn't thought you'd ever want to leave Stoney Brook."

"I don't think I've ever been to a place that made me want to consider it. There's just something about Ireland that calls to me. Makes me want to spend more time here and learn all I can about this beautiful country."

Billie turned to look at me, his eyes wide. "I never in a million years thought I'd hear those words from your lips. You're a Mainer to the core."

"But my roots are here. Just like you said, it's the mother-land." I smiled at my words, too happy to hold back. "Now, do you think we should call that distributor and see if they can get some lobster? I know we don't have the rolls made, but I thought we could get it all ready and make it tomorrow."

"Sure, we can. Let me call Joseph and get the information."

I listened while Billie talked to him like he'd known him forever, and as he laughed at whatever he heard on the other end of the line, the warm feeling in my chest grew. I reached for his hand and held it while he kept talking. Asking about how work was, and what Joseph had planned for dinner.

"So, Lance was thinking we could start some dough for lobster rolls tonight, then tomorrow we'll cook our specialty. What do you think?" Billie put the phone on speaker and winked at me.

"You boys are the best. I'd love that. Just tell me what you need, and I'll make sure we have it."

"Can I get the distributors' information from you? I want to order the lobster," I said.

Joseph answered with a hearty laugh. "Well, I can't say no to that now, can I."

Billie dialed the number Joseph gave him and after a short negotiation, Billie thanked the man he spoke to before hanging up. "He said we can swing by on the way to Castlecomer today, but if we don't make it there by the time he closes, he'll deliver it to Joseph's in the morning."

"Thanks, Billie. How about we let them deliver it tomorrow? We can focus on making the rolls and spend a little time with Joseph, before going back to the hotel for a quiet dinner. I think I'd really like to spend a quiet evening with my boyfriend."

"You're so sweet, and while I'd really like a quiet evening with *my* boyfriend, I think you should spend as much time with Joseph as you can. Why don't we go prep everything we can this afternoon, and spend a little time with him, then we can go back to the hotel, and hang out at the pub, and have a quiet night." Billie smiled and squeezed my hand.

"I love you. There are not even words for me to tell you how much you mean to me, but I'll spend the rest of my life trying." I pulled his hand to my lips and kissed it. His eyes softened as he watched my every move before forcing his eyes back to the road.

"I-I think I'd really like that." He cleared his throat, but his eyes never left me.

We drove around a while longer and stopped for snacks at a few places along the way back to the hotel. It was a beautiful day, and we enjoyed everything we came across. Something I'd never let myself do.

As we pulled into town and drove past Joseph's café, he was just stepping outside to bring in his specials board. He threw his hand up in the air and gave us a big wave. We laughed and waved back. "Let's go over right now and see if he minds if we get started on the rolls. We need to check he has all the ingredients anyway."

Billie nodded as I pulled into a parking space behind our hotel. "That sounds great. Are you sure you don't want to spend more time with Joseph tonight?"

"No, I want to make tomorrow night a special meal, but I meant what I said. I want to spend tonight with you." I turned in the seat and faced Billie. "You make my life so much more than what it was before you. I really need to send my nephew a monthly gift card for flaking on me that day." He smiled at my words, as I brushed my knuckle against the slight stubble on his cheek.

"Come on, Romeo, let's go say hello to Joseph and see if it's too busy before we end up back in the room for the evening. Not that I'd mind," Billie said.

"Yep, let's go. It won't take long to get the rolls ready, but I feel bad using his supplies. Maybe we need to give him—"

"Lance," Billie interrupted. "Did you not notice how excited he was when you were talking to him about it? Maybe slip him a little money before we leave. But since he's related to you, I can't see him taking it. Might be better to give it to his wife."

"Somehow, I think she's probably just as stubborn as he is," I mumbled.

"Well, you have to be a little stubborn to put up with someone else who's stubborn. And yes, Lance, I mean you," Billie said, before bending over laughing.

"Billie—" I started before stopping myself. He was right, and he knew it as well as I did. Without another word, I pulled him close and kissed him. "Come on, let's go see what trouble we can get into."

Sixteen

Time

Billie

We talked to Joseph, and he was as excited as we were about making the lobster rolls. "Go have some time to yourself, and when you're ready to start on them, just come back over. I'll be closing around six and I'll be here cleaning and working on my inventory."

"No family dinner tonight?" Lance asked.

"Not tonight, but they'll all be knocking on the door tomorrow night. Every relative in the immediate area will be here." Joseph laughed and welcomed a customer in before turning back to us. "Are you still here? Go on now, I'll see you two later."

We walked back toward the hotel, but Lance tugged me along past it. "Let's go look at this bridge."

We walked past the hotel to a path that led to the bridge we'd driven over when we first arrived. Adjacent to the old bridge was a recently built pedestrian bridge. The main bridge was barely wide enough for two vehicles, and walking on the path next to it, its age was apparent. Under the main bridge which stood over a shallow creek, were three arches, all of it made of roughhewn stone.

"Wow, this is beautiful," I said as we walked across to the other side. A plaque said the main bridge was far older than anything back home, and I tried to imagine what it looked like in years past when Castlecomer was a small village.

The breeze was warm today, and the sun tried to peek through the clouds enough to brighten the gloom of the past day. We stopped in the middle as we crossed back, and for a while, neither of us spoke. It was enough to be standing next to the love of my life.

"Why don't we go explore town a little more?" I asked.

"That sounds good. We've got plenty of time," Lance said. When we first arrived, he'd struggled with slowing down and just enjoying all the new experiences we were having. But now he wanted to see everything he could. The time was going way too fast, and there was still so much to see. And I wanted to make sure he saw it all.

Past the hotel was a post office, a secondhand shop, and a small grocery store. "Let's go get some snacks," I said, and the two of us walked in. There was a big display of ready to go foods that we both considered before choosing sandwiches.

"I noticed a park across the street. Why don't we take this and go eat there? It's a nice day out, and I'm liking having a little time with you all alone. Driving doesn't count," Lance said, as I picked something else to snack on.

"I think that's a great idea. Let's see what else we can find, and we'll go check it out."

A few minutes later, we were walking out with a bag full of food and heading towards the park. The grass was green and inviting, but it was also wet, so after finding a table, we sat down to eat. Lance had a serious look on his face, and I wanted to ask him what he was thinking about, but I didn't want to pry. He squeezed my hand and explained before I could ask.

"I've had such an odd feeling since meeting Joseph. I instantly knew we were related, and I loved meeting his family.

My family. And for reasons I can't explain, I felt so close to this country I'd never visited before, and I knew deep in my bones I would never forget the mix of emotions I've had while we've been here. I'm so glad we're sharing this together."

"I know what you mean." I may have come here a stranger, who had reached out to a man I'd never talked to before, but I was now a family member same as Lance. "After one evening, I count all of Joseph's family as my own, and a part of me now wants to claim Ireland as a part of me, too," I said.

This far away land we'd never set foot in until a few days ago, that we now felt as comfortable in as though we were at home. It was weird and wonderful, and somehow comforting at the same time. Knowing the part of me that connected me to this country, and Lance to his relatives, was happy and fulfilled, and gave me peace. Ireland filled my heart.

I took out the food we'd chosen and handed Lance his sandwich. "What's got you thinking so hard over there?"

"Just thinking about lobster rolls," he lied with a grin.

"Okay, okay, let's eat and then we'll go get started," I said, and rolled my eyes before smiling. "I like Irish Lance."

"Lance has always been Irish." He laughed before taking a bite. I didn't say a word. Just took a bite as he smiled at me like he was in on the biggest secret and he loved it. We finished eating and stayed a while longer at the park. It was beautiful, and it forced Lance to slow down more than he had in far too many years.

A text alert got my attention, and I took out my phone to check. Reading it, I laughed before showing it to Lance.

"Get yer arse over here and start cooking," Lance read out loud in a fairly good Irish accent.

"It is so obvious you two are related," I said, and started putting everything away.

"Well? You ready?" He held his hand out and I took it. Since the park was right behind Joseph's café, we walked directly there.

The closed sign was up, but the door was unlocked, so we walked in, and as soon as we closed the door behind us, Joseph came out of the kitchen.

"Well? Come on then, let's get these rolls baked." He stood with his hands on his hips, apron still on, and hair a mess from raking his hands through it all day.

"Let's go," Lance said, and Joseph slapped him on the back.

"I think I got everything you need. The distributor confirmed the lobster will be delivered tomorrow, and I've invited everyone I know," Joseph rambled as we walked into the kitchen.

He'd set up everything at a short counter for us to use, which reminded me so much of the food truck, and the three of us worked together to measure and mix the dough. When it was time to portion it all out, we all worked together on that, too.

"Do you think this is enough?" Lance asked after I slid the fourth full tray of rolls into the rack to rise before we baked them.

"How many people did you invite?" I asked Joseph.

He squinted his eye as he looked up at the ceiling at some invisible math problem he was working out in his head. "I invited around fifty, but most of them are going to stop by and take a roll to go. I hope you don't mind, but everyone is curious about my American relative."

Now it was Lance doing calculations in his head while I counted all the rolls again. "I think we're okay, but why don't we make one more tray just in case? It can't hurt to have too many."

"Good thing you ordered too much lobster," Joseph said.

"Good thing," Lance said, and they grinned at each other.

The three of us had another smaller batch done and ready to rise. I made sure the oven was ready before he put the first tray in to bake. Soon the familiar smell of fresh bread filled the kitchen with the scent of Lance's famous rolls.

As soon as they were done, I gingerly picked one up and tore a piece off for Joseph.

"You make me proud to be related to ya," he said with a grin as he sampled the delicious bread. "These are nearly as good as the sourdough."

Those words meant so much to Lance, and I knew it was partially in jest, but it didn't matter. I leaned my head against his shoulder. He had found his happiness, and it showed.

Seventeen
Good Times

LANCE

We'd finished the rolls around midnight, but the energy in the kitchen was still high. And even though we were done way later than I expected us to be, I wasn't ready to leave.

"Lance, go. I can finish cleaning up here," Joseph said, as he wiped down the counter we'd used to knead the dough.

"I don't mind. It's been nice working with someone else in the kitchen."

"Thanks, Lance," Billie said, and flung a towel at my head.

"You know what I mean. I barely let Billie help the day we met, and it was only because I was desperate. But working together with him has always been one of my favorite things." I pulled him in close and kissed his cheek.

"It has been fun baking together. Tomorrow we'll make the lobster mix, and your family will get to taste what Lance is famous for." Billie's eyes shone with pride and love. It was easy for me to see, and when Joseph looked between the two of us, his smile, followed by a wink, told me he saw it too.

"I'm so happy you both came to visit. It's been lots of fun getting to know you two. Even if you are slightly obsessed with cooking," Joseph said and laughed.

"Must be genetic," I said.

"It's got to be," Joseph said, and slapped me on the back. "Go back to your hotel and relax. Tomorrow we'll plan dinner around six in the evening. That should give everyone time to get here, and us time to get it all ready."

"That sounds great. We can find plenty to explore early in the day," Billie said.

"Yes, we can, and I can't wait to see what else we find." I meant it. In the span of a few days, I'd gone from someone who wasn't all that interested in playing tourist to someone who wanted to see all that Ireland offered.

"Then off with you," Joseph said, and after a quick hug, we were out the door.

"So, what are we going to see tomorrow?" I asked Billie.

"Well, there are a few things I think you'd like. We can go see where they make Waterford China, or there's a Titanic Museum and a few castles."

"Let's see it all. I mean, as much as we can and still make it back here on time. I think as long as we're at the restaurant by five, we should have plenty of time to make the lobster mix. What do you think?"

"Sleep first?" Billie said and took my hand as we crossed the street.

"Well, maybe something else first." I pulled him close and kissed his neck at the door to the hotel. "Come on."

When we returned to the room, neither of us hurried to go to bed, and when we were at last under the covers, both of us seemed content to enjoy the warmth of being so close.

"Is there anything you absolutely want to see while we're here?" Billie asked.

"No, I'm enjoying everywhere you've taken me so far."

"We have an idea now about what's nearby, so if we don't see it all tomorrow, for sure we can go the next day."

Our time here was coming to an end, and I knew Billie felt responsible for us not missing a thing, but he'd already given me everything I needed on this trip.

"We can do that, but there's nothing that will mean more to me than spending time with Joseph and his family. It really has been a lot of fun." We were both on our sides facing each other, and I once again thanked the fates for putting him in my path. He brushed his thumb across my cheek before I took his hand in mine and held it to my chest.

"We can come back again, you know. It could even be a yearly tradition," Billie said, his eyes sparkling with happiness, and a soft smile playing on his lips.

"Maybe next time we can stay longer."

His eyes widened. "Do you mean it? There's so much more to see. We've barely explored one small area."

"I do. At first, I was so worried about missing work, but you were right about everything. Mom has kept me up on the business, and it's all going smoothly. I think if we hire someone and train them, they could take care of it while we're gone."

Billie's eyes widened again. "You're serious? Because I never in a million years thought I'd hear you saying we should plan to take time off. I think maybe this vacation thing is wearing off on you."

I rolled over and pinned him under me while he beamed up at me. Taking his lips in a sweet kiss, I thought of all the times I'd chosen work, over spending time with him, and I made a promise to myself that would change. Billie was my home, and I wanted him to know how special he was to me, and how much I loved our time together. "I'm serious. But I'll expect you to help me train this person. They'll need to be able to work with us both and be self-reliant enough to not need us."

"I like that idea. Spending more time with you outside work would be great."

"Let's plan to come here again next year. I'd like to be able to tell Joseph before we leave."

"He'll be thrilled to hear that, and who knows, maybe you two can do something together outside his kitchen," Billie said, with a laugh.

"Maybe. And maybe you and I need to do the same. I love you for more than your work ethic, you know." I brushed his hair back from his forehead. It was getting longer since we'd been here. He'd shaved it short not long before we'd left and I'd loved the look and feel of it, but the way it looked now reminded me how he'd looked when we first met.

"I know, and I love you for so many things that don't actually involve work. One of them is the way you're looking at me now. I can feel the love in your gaze," he whispered.

I kissed him then, and all talk of work and vacation was forgotten as we settled into touching each other and making love like it was the first time all over again. Work was important to me, and before I'd met Billie it was my life, but now he was my everything, and I didn't want to wake up one day and regret not spending more time with him.

"I love you, Billie," I whispered, pulling him close and settling into his side.

"I love you too," he whispered back as his breaths evened out and he fell asleep in my arms. There wasn't another person who would ever be as perfect for me as he was. I'd found my other half, and I'd always do my best to make sure we ended every day in each other's arms.

Eighteen

Lobster Rolls

BILLIE

Seeing Ireland through the eyes of the man I love was even better than experiencing it myself. Lance probably hadn't noticed how much he paid attention to every small detail now, when at first, he'd ignored most of the sites we'd gone to in Dublin, and tried to act like he enjoyed it. Now he savored it all, from the hotel we'd stayed in, to the bridge we'd driven over several times now.

"What's on the agenda for today?" he asked, as we ate breakfast at the hotel. We'd be spending the latter part of the day with his family, so to get an early start we opted to eat here today.

"Well, I thought we could start with the Titanic Museum and decide what we want to do next."

"That sounds great, it looks like there's a lot to do around there."

"Yes, and I'm really enjoying seeing it all by car. Think of all the things we've seen along the way. I mean besides the type of mortar they used to build the walls along the side of the road," I said, making Lance laugh.

"I'm getting better at driving. Yesterday wasn't so bad, was it?"

He was so sweet and seeing him enjoy himself was something I wanted to soak up while we were here. I kissed his cheek and nuzzled his neck before I answered. "I think you're doing a great job. I admit it's something I wouldn't have wanted to try."

We finished eating and were waiting for a cup of coffee to go before we'd decided on a few things we wanted to do that were all in the same area as the museum.

"I like the idea of going to Waterford. I noticed we'll drive through Kilkenny again," Lance said.

"Okay then that's what we'll do. I know we can find lots of things to do along the way, and if we see something interesting, we can pull off and check it out." Our coffees were ready, and we were in the car driving the same route we'd driven yesterday while I googled as he drove and hummed along to the radio to a random song I'd never heard. It felt so familiar to be driving around in a different country and enjoying it all. And if the smile on Lance's face told me anything, I'd say he felt the same way.

We chatted most of the way there, and after finding a parking space we walked around the downtown area before deciding where we'd go. After two museums, a cathedral, and two more cups of coffee we were both ready to go back to Castlecomer.

"Let's see if we can find dessert to share with everyone," Lance said as we walked past a small bakery. After deciding on a cake that the baker assured us would be the best we'd ever had, we were back on the road headed to the hotel.

"Are you ready for this?" I asked Lance as we drove through town.

"I think so, but I'm glad we're back early. I think I'll go see if Joseph has room to store the cake."

"Go ahead. I'll take everything up to the room and meet you there."

"You're sure you don't mind?" He looked at me like a kid who'd been told he could go play with his friends instead of doing chores, and it was absolutely adorable.

"I'm sure." He parked the car behind the hotel and after a quick kiss, he jogged off toward the café with the cake he'd bought. I hurried to the room and dropped everything off before joining Lance.

The closed sign was on the door, but I could see Lance and Joseph inside. They were on opposite sides of the worktable, and Lance was showing Joseph how we prepared the lobster. I stood at the door and watched the two of them. Both so similar, yet not, and both so happy to have the other in their life. Joseph had made such a big impression on Lance, and I hoped he meant it when he said we'd come back here next year.

Joseph turned around and after doing a doubletake he walked over to the door, wiping his hands off on his apron as he approached.

"Hey, what are you doing all the way out here? Come on now, there's work to be done." He clapped his hand on my shoulder as I passed him on the way to where Lance was. He was busy chopping the celery, and I gathered the rest of the ingredients while he finished. Joseph watched every detail, taking note of all the steps and asking questions when he wasn't sure. It didn't take us long to get the big bowl of filling ready to go, and right after that there was a knock at the door.

"I hope you two are ready. The whole family's gonna be here, and they can eat," Joseph said, and nodded to the door.

"We're used to it," I said, and he laughed before he opened the door with a dramatic bow.

"Welcome, everyone. Get ready for the best damn lobster rolls you've ever had. Courtesy of my nephew Lance and his guy Billie." He winked at us as people we hadn't met yet walked in and went right to a table. "Just make yourself at home."

"Oh, we plan to," an older woman said, as she and a few other people sat down.

Joseph laughed and welcomed them all. Another knock at the door and he was off to open it again; this time it was his wife, Annie, and everyone we'd met the other night. "Go on, love, help Lance," his wife said, and shooed him off in our direction.

"Let's go ahead and get them going. The sooner we feed them the more they'll settle down." Joseph watched as Lance set several rolls on a tray to toast and waited for the first ones to be done. As soon as they were ready, I put each of them on a plate before loading the roll with the lobster mix.

Joseph put a bag of chips on the plate, and asked everyone what they wanted to drink when he took them their food. It didn't take long for their reaction to echo around the room.

"Hey, Joseph, you're adding this to the menu, right?" a young man at one of the tables asked.

"I just might, Liam. But for now, you need to thank your cousin for sharing his fabulous cooking. He's famous for these back in the States. Did you know that?" Joseph bragged. He knew Lance's story but neither of us minded if he played it up a bit.

"You better get that recipe, mate," the young man said before shoving half of the roll into his mouth.

"We'll see," Joseph said.

Lance smiled, busy as ever and loving every minute of it. Doing what he loved to do the most. Sharing his delicious food with the ones he loved. And even though most of the people in the small café were strangers he hadn't met yet; they were his family.

Nineteen

More

LANCE

Billie and I worked together as flawlessly as always, and Joseph blended in with us in a way few could match. He seated everyone, and if I hadn't met them yet, he brought them to the kitchen and introduced them.

"Doing great, Lance. Thanks again for sharing your specialty with us all," Joseph said, and clapped me on the back. Billie stood right behind him, and the happiness shining in his eyes made Joseph's words much more powerful and meaningful to me. Maybe it was the fact we were crammed into a tiny kitchen not meant for three cooks at a time, or maybe it was knowing there were relatives out in the dining room I'd never dreamed of, let alone imagined I'd meet. Either way, it all was wonderful, and in a way, life changing.

"How many more do you expect?" I asked Joseph.

"They're all here. We can finish it all up and go sit and visit." He put the rest of the rolls on a tray and got them ready to toast while Billie and I portioned out the remaining lobster mix. After we'd finished, the two of us both started cleaning, which was our normal routine.

Joseph's lips lifted in a sideways grin. "You two really are a great team."

"Yeah, we are, we kick ass," Billie said, and attempted a high five that we both missed and laughed about.

"Lance, come out here, lad. I want you to meet the rest of the family," someone called from the dining room.

"Well, go on then," Joseph said. "I can finish in here."

Billie and I took off our aprons and set them on the counter before walking into the other room. It was packed, every seat taken and lots of loud, cheerful conversations rang out around the small room. Everyone seemed to look up at the same time as soon as we were out of the kitchen, and they all wanted us to sit at their table. Billie took my hand and tugged me to the one with Joseph's wife, Annie. She reintroduced us to everyone seated with her. Some we'd already met and others who we'd never seen.

"Tell me about yourselves," an older man said, who was seated at the next table.

"This is Ryan. He's Joseph's great-uncle, so I suppose somewhere down the line he's yours too," Annie explained. She was a small woman with shoulder-length grey hair and beautiful blue eyes and every time she looked in Joseph's direction his eyes found hers.

"Do you live in Castlecomer too?" Billie asked, already falling into an easy conversation with him.

"Yes, just down the road. It's where I grew up from the time I was a small child and it'll probably be where I'll die," Ryan said.

"It's beautiful here. I can understand not leaving. Why look for perfection when you've already found it?" Billie said.

Ryan looked between Billie and me before speaking. "How long have you two been together?"

"A few years now. Once I met Billie, I knew there was never going to be anyone else for me."

"You can see your love for each other written all over your faces. You two best make the most of that love. Don't ever squander it," Ryan said, his voice taking on a serious quality.

"Ryan lost his partner a few years back. He fell ill and never recovered," Annie said and covered his hand with hers.

"Sorry for your loss," Billie said, and lay his hand on Ryan's arm.

Ryan patted it with his other wrinkled hand. "There now. This is a time for celebration and new beginnings. It's not every day we get to meet such a fine long-lost relative as Lance and you, his Billie."

"I want to hear more about this partner of yours," Billie said.

"Tell me what you want to know," Ryan said with a smile, and the two of them talked softly amongst themselves for a time.

"So, are you keen on moving here yet?" Joseph asked and slid into the chair next to me.

"I'd love to, but I can't see how that would work with our business. We're just getting it to the place we want it to be. And you know I couldn't be an absentee owner, leaving it in the hands of someone else full time."

"No, I don't suppose you would." Joseph scratched his chin while he spoke. "I know we'd talked about me coming to visit, but what would you think of planning that out while you're still here? I'd love to see your business, and your mum's too."

"Hell yes," Billie said, making Joseph laugh.

"Then let's make it happen. I'm sure I have enough family that can run this place while we go visit and learn more about the mysterious American cousins."

"You can count on me, Uncle Joseph," a young man shouted from another table.

"That's quite alright, Liam. I'd sooner ask one of the strangers that come through here than you," Joseph said with a smile.

Not taking any offense, Liam threw his head back and laughed before raising his pint in cheers. "You might be right about that, Joseph."

"How much longer are you here?" Ryan asked.

"Our plane leaves early Sunday," Billie said.

"If you get the chance, why don't you stop by. I'd love to have you for a visit."

"How about tomorrow?" I asked and looked at Billie for reassurance.

"That would be great. We haven't made plans yet. How do you feel about going for a ride? We have a rental car and I know Lance would love you to come and join us. We're just driving around the area seeing what we can see," Billie explained.

"I'd like that. It's been a while since I've gone outside the city limits." Ryan laughed at his own words.

"We could go see King John's Castle. Would you be willing to go that far? It says it's a ninety-minute drive," Billie asked while looking at his phone.

"I'd love to. They've excavated more and added to the museum since I've been there last," Ryan said.

"How long ago was that?" I asked.

"Several years ago. They're always working on it, so it's always changing. But it's a very interesting castle to explore."

"Then it's a date. Tomorrow we'll all go to King John's Castle," Billie said.

"Just tell me what time I need to be ready. I live quite close to the café, so I can meet you here if you'd like," Ryan said.

"We can pick you up. Then we'll grab something for breakfast on the drive." We'd slipped into a routine of breakfast before going, but I wanted to enjoy as much time with Ryan as I could. Meeting and spending time with another relative was perfect in my eyes.

More family, more friends, more chances to meet people I was related to, and I didn't want to waste any opportunity to spend time with any of them one on one. But the sadness that covered Ryan was hard to miss, and I found myself wanting to know more about his partner and the life they'd had before his passing. My eyes met Billie's and I couldn't imagine a world without him in it. I didn't need to ask if he felt the same. I knew it in my bones.

More time with the most important person in the world to me was all I needed to truly be happy.

Twenty

Ryan

BILLIE

I leaned in close as Ryan spoke. If I had to guess, I'd say he was in his sixties, but he looked far older than that. He overflowed with sadness and hurt.

"How long were you together?" I asked.

"We met when we were in our twenties, so around forty years, I suppose." Ryan's eyes got a little misty at his words, and I suspected he knew exactly how long it was.

"Is that how long it was?" a woman with short gray hair asked and patted him on the hand.

"Yes, Fi, I met him when I was working in Dublin."

"Oh, that's right. I'd forgotten about your jaded past," she joked. "I'm Fiona, by the way, I'm Joseph's auntie."

"Nice to meet you, Fiona, I'm Billie and this is—"

"Lance, yes, I know. Joseph has talked about nothing but the two of you since you arrived. Thank you so much for spending some time here with him. I think it's breathed some fresh life into him. Not like he needed help. That boy has more energy than three people." She laughed as she glanced at Joseph, who was still running from table to table.

"It's the same for Lance. He loved meeting all of his family," I whispered as I leaned in closer to her. Lance was still focused on Joseph, and I knew he was forcing himself not to help him.

"Lance is a sweet man. I'm glad to see he's got you," she said with a gentle smile.

I cleared my throat before speaking, overcome with emotions once again on this trip. "Ryan's going to go explore with us tomorrow. We still have more we want to see."

"Oh, Ryan, it'll be good for you to get out. These two have been all over the place. I've been seeing the pictures they post on their business page on Facebook," Fiona said.

"You looked at our page?" Lance asked her as he gathered up some empty plates from our table.

"Of course I did. It's nice to keep up on what the family is doing," Fi explained before Lance rushed off to the kitchen.

"I'm excited to go. I told them it's been a while since I've been outside the city limits," Ryan said with a grin.

"What do you have planned?" she asked.

"We're going to see King John's Castle. I want to see as many castles as we can, and there's a lot around that area to explore."

"Ryan and Jamie used to go to every old building they could find. Isn't that right, Ryan?"

It was the first time someone had mentioned his partner's name, and I didn't miss the wave of hurt that passed over Ryan at his mention.

"We loved seeing the history of our country. There was so much to discover right in this area. Jamie was from the north, so all of this was new to him, and he loved every bit he learned." Ryan's eyes took on a faraway look as he spoke, and I wondered if he was remembering times they'd spent together.

"Lance didn't think he'd like it, but now he's looking forward to seeing more. I predict more vacations to Ireland in our future."

"Oh, that's great," Fiona said, and clapped her hands. "You two have really made an impression on the family. Most of this lot hasn't gotten together like this in years. Apparently, we only needed to offer free food for them to join us." She yelled that last part and looked pointedly at a few guests, who quickly looked away.

Lance stopped by the table long enough to kiss my cheek before he was doing the same as Joseph was and checking on each table. Blood or not, they were both cut from the same cloth, and the longer we spent time with Lance's family, the more that was clear.

The next morning, we met Ryan at Joseph's café because he insisted, he was just fine walking. He looked a little nervous as we strode up, but after we all had a coffee and a little to eat, he was relaxed and ready to go.

"I thought we could go right to the castle, then we can see what else there is in the area. How does that sound?" Lance asked.

"Sounds great," I said.

"There's a lot to be found there. I'll try to remember the best parts," Ryan said, as the three of us settled into the car.

We chatted as Lance drove, and Ryan told us more about himself. "I've always loved history, so much so that I studied to be an archaeologist. There's just so much of the past right here. I wanted to understand more of what I was seeing."

"I noticed how many buildings are in ruin along the roads. It must be amazing living so close to so many areas where history was made," I said.

"Yes, it is. I can't think of anyplace else I'd rather live," Ryan said.

"I'm beginning to feel the same way. I've always lived in Stoney Brook, but seeing this part of the world has been enlightening. It doesn't hurt that I've got to spend time with more family than I ever imagined I would have," Lance said, and reached across the console for my hand.

We pulled into the city of Limerick, where King John's Castle was located. It looked a lot like the other towns we'd driven through. Houses all set close together, and businesses with colorful storefronts. The castle was nearby, so Lance drove right there. The area surrounding it was mostly businesses, and lots of souvenir shops. "This looks like a big tourist area," he said.

"That it is," Ryan said.

We'd left early, so when we pulled into the parking area, we were the only car there. I looked around for a sign that would say it was open soon because it looked like it was still closed. "Did you check the hours?" I asked.

"Yes, we're a few minutes early," Lance said, and the three of us got out of the car. We walked over to the entrance area, and I hoped someone would show up soon. Just as the thought crossed my mind, a man about Ryan's age opened the inner door and slid open the small window next to the entrance.

"Good morning, did you want to go inside?" he asked in a very British accent. He looked past me to Ryan, and his eyes widened in shock. "Ryan Doyle?"

"Gerald, it's been a minute," Ryan said, and grinned.

"Wait, you two know each other?" I asked.

"You could say that," Gerald said from inside the booth with the same grin Ryan wore. "Well, are you coming in or not?"

"Oh, we're going in," Lance said, and paid for our admission.

We walked through the door to find Gerald waiting there for us. "Mind if I take you on a tour?"

"Not at all," Ryan said, and the two of them walked ahead of us.

"What just happened?" Lance asked.

"I think your great-uncle just used us to get a date," I said to him. Ryan turned back to us and this time he wore a bright smile and had a twinkle in his eye. The wink he shot us didn't surprise me, but it did make me laugh.

Lance took my hand and squeezed it. "That'll be us some-day," he whispered as the two men leaned in close to talk.

Twenty-One
Old Things

Lance

We followed them through the museum that was at the beginning of the tour. Gerald pointed out unique items that, to him, were of great historical significance. It was surprising and incredible that so much had survived through the years. But more amazing was seeing the way Ryan's eyes lit up with every word.

"So, Ryan tells me you're a long-lost relative," Gerald said as he walked next to me, his hands clutched behind his back and a warm smile on his face. Billie and Ryan walked ahead of us and read every plaque on the walls.

"Yes, Billie set this all up. I had no clue I had so many relatives here. I knew my family had come from Ireland a long time ago, but I guess I never thought there were still so many of them here."

"You've a big family here. Probably even more in other counties."

"I bet you're right. Every time we've gotten together with Joseph's family, there seems to be a few more."

"Thank you for taking Ryan out with you today. I know you probably didn't want to take an old man out sightseeing, but

I also know how much he enjoys the history of our country, and how long ago it's been since he's left Castlecomer."

"I only just met him, but he seems very nice. I was sorry to hear he'd lost his husband. It sounds like they'd been together a long time."

"Yes, they'd been together for years. We were all friends at one time, did you know that?" Gerald asked.

"No, we were all talking last night at Joseph's café. Billie and I mentioned we were coming here today to see the castle, and he asked if we minded if he rode along."

"Did he now?" Gerald smiled at his own words, but I wasn't sure what was going on between the two of them. "I haven't seen him for more than twenty years. The three of us got into a fight one night. I don't remember what it was about. But after that, I never saw either of them again. We used to have so many adventures. All of us shared the same love of history and worked on a few archeological digs." His eyes held a far-off dreamy look, and a fondness that told of old friends long forgotten but remembered again.

"Maybe you two can start spending time together again? I get the feeling he's a little bored sitting home all the time."

Billie turned to look at me with a grin. "We're going into the castle now. Are you ready?" he asked.

"The museum ends here and leads directly into the main castle. It's beautiful and surprisingly well preserved," Gerald explained.

"You'll be joining us, won't you?" Ryan asked him.

"Of course. I wouldn't miss showing you all the new excavation for the world." Gerald winked at me before taking Ryan's arm and leading him toward the door that led the way. "All of this is actually part of the castle, but they converted it into a museum, and gave it a more modern look so that when you entered the actual castle, you were immersed into that world."

"Wow," Billie said as soon as he was through the door.

The rough-hewn stone walls were similar to the other castles we'd been to, but this one was different. The stones were heavier and fortified, more like a fort than anything we'd been to yet. Walking through a large wooden door, we walked outside to a immense courtyard. It had been made to look like it did when this was still being used. Complete with a blacksmith's shop, an archery field, and a large open area that had probably at one time been a market.

Billie walked over to where I stood and took my hand. "Come on, let's see what's over there." He pointed to the far end of the courtyard, and after Ryan waved us on, we walked in that direction. "This is amazing."

"*You're* amazing. This is just another thing you've shown me that reveals more of the land my relatives came from." I kissed the side of his head. "Let's go see where this goes."

We walked past another heavy wooden door that led down a hall. At the end was a spiral staircase that we climbed. It wound around and around until it led out to the top of the castle and to a narrow walkway that faced the sea. "Do you think this castle saw battles?" I asked.

"I think they all did, but this one has been modified several times. When they excavated it, they found it was fortified each time it fell in battle." We hurried along across the top and looked down at the area we'd just been in. Off to the side, Gerald and Ryan sat, their heads so close they nearly touched. It was easy to see how much each of them cared for the other, and how much they'd missed each other.

"Let's let them have more time to catch up," I said, and Billie wrapped his arms around me from behind.

"Have I told you lately how much I love you?" he whispered in my ear.

I caressed his arm with my hand and leaned back into his warmth. "Only a few times, but I don't think I'll ever get tired of hearing it."

"I love you," he whispered before nibbling on my ear.

"I love you too. I never would have believed it was possible to love anyone as much as I love you. You're my heart, and my home." I'd said these things to him many times. But I'd tell him every day of my life and it still wouldn't be enough. I'd spent most of my life with my head down working hard and letting life do with me what it would. But not anymore.

"You're the best thing that ever happened to me, Lance. I know you probably don't believe that, but it's true." Billie's voice cracked as he spoke, making my throat tighten with emotion.

"There's no one else in this world I'd rather live this life with than you," I said as I spun around and pulled him into my arms. "Marry me, Billie. I know we've talked about it before. But marry me here, in Ireland. Getting married here feels right." We swayed back and forth as we held each other tight, and when he realized what I'd said, he gasped.

"Are you serious?"

"Billie, you know me better than anyone else. Do you think I'd joke about something like that?"

Twenty-Two
This is Real

BILLIE

He was serious. I could see it in his eyes and hear it in the way his voice quivered. I knew deep down in my heart we'd always be together, and I hoped we would marry. But it wasn't something I worried about or gave too much thought to. We'd talked about it many times, but mostly in a what-if-this-happened kinda way.

"You know I don't need a piece of paper and a ring to bind my life with yours. You're everything to me." Now it was my voice that quivered and while I told myself it was that this was happening at a castle in Ireland, I knew it was because all of this was real.

"I know that baby, but I love you, and I want everyone to know how I feel. Marrying you would be the easiest thing for me to do and would make me so happy." His thumb brushed against my cheek and the warmth in his eyes took my breath away. He meant every word he said.

"You really want to get married here?"

"Yes, I really do. I can call Mom and your family, and anyone who wants to come is welcome. We'll need to stay a little longer. Do you suppose that would be a problem? I know we mentioned staying longer, but I didn't really consider it at the time. Do you think we can still take the extra week off?" Lance rattled things off and I could see he was now committed to it happening.

"What do we do first?" I asked. His excitement was contagious, and when I glanced down at Ryan and Gerald to find them smiling up at us, I knew it was all too perfect.

He pulled out his phone and took a picture of us. We both looked a little maniacal, with wide smiles and excitement in our eyes. He then tapped out a message and sent it to our families and any friends we could think of. He'd barely pressed send when incoming messages started sounding.

"What do they say?" I asked and tried to read his phone.

"It doesn't matter, we're getting married!" he shouted those last words over the wall.

Ryan and Gerald both laughed and waved at us from below. I hoped they both found half the happiness in each other that I found in Lance's arms. "You're both invited," I yelled down to them.

"What do we do now?" Lance asked.

"Now we figure out where we'll be doing this, and how we'll feed everyone."

"Well, the food won't be an issue. I wonder if that park behind Joseph's café allows weddings?"

I pictured the beautiful green park we'd walked past several times now. With its lush green grass surrounded by trees that seemed to block out the modern world in that little slice of heaven. "That's a great idea, and maybe we can hire Joseph to do the food. I don't want either of us to be busy cooking before the ceremony. We need to focus on each other," I said and leaned in close to him.

"I can't wait to call you my husband," Lance murmured. His thumb brushed my cheek and his eyes shone with more love than I ever thought possible.

"What about rings? I mean, we want rings, don't we?" In two seconds, I'd gone from bliss to panic. Where would we get rings on such short notice? Was that even a possibility?

"How about we ask Ryan and Gerald if there's a jewelry store they can recommend? We could go today and pick out rings. I mean, if you want to," he said, some of his previous excitement fading with the touch of reality.

"Lance, there's nothing I want more. I do have one request."

"Whatever you want, I don't mind."

"I want us to get traditional Irish wedding rings. It only seems right. Our love has only grown in this magical place, and I don't ever want to forget that. Oh, and we'll need to reschedule our flight home and see if the hotel has openings for another week." Our list of things to do kept growing, but like we always did, we considered every decision together.

"The rings sound perfect, and I'm sure Ryan will have an idea where to go. I'll check on the airline. You look into the hotel. Do you think a week more is long enough?"

"We'd planned for a week longer just in case, but we'll know more after we talk to Joseph. Do you think your mom will mind? I don't want to cut it short, but I also don't want to put too much on her."

At my words, Lance looked down at a text he'd received. "It's from Mom. She says she's hired a new manager, that they were doing a great job already and she knows they can handle it while we're gone. She says she expected us to want to stay longer, and to take as long as we need to, and she'll be here when we give her a date." He smiled as he read it, and I knew everything was happening the way it was supposed to. We were meant to be.

"Oh, and the rest of the family will be there, too." Another text got his attention, and he read it too. "Your dad said he's been waiting to hear from us. He knew we'd be getting married soon." Lance's eyes were a little misty as he read. I knew he'd worried what my family would think of him, but they had accepted him from the start. His hard work and dedication were both traits my family valued.

"I wonder if they'll really show up. They keep saying they'll visit but haven't made it yet." I thought of all the times they told me they'd spend some time with us in Stoney Brook then ended up not making it. Just as my mood started to sour, my phone signaled a text. Laughing, I showed it to Lance. "My dad said not to worry about the food, they'll pay for whatever we want."

"See, babe, it's meant to be." His phone sounded with yet another alert and with a kiss to my cheek, he read it. "It's from Mom. She said she's paying for a band, a location, or anything we need. It seems like she and your family had already planned what they'd provide." Lance smiled as he read the message again.

"Sounds like they're as happy as we are," I whispered.

"Sounds like it," he said, and pulled me close again. "I can't wait to tell Joseph." He grinned as he met my eyes.

"Lance, I have a feeling this isn't going to be a small affair. His family is huge, and you know they'll all want to go. I hope you're ready for that." I was serious. He wasn't one to make a big deal of things or be the person in a crowd demanding attention. Lance preferred to blend in and do as he wished, with no one judging him for his choices.

"I know. But I'm proud to be marrying the man I love in the land where my family began, and I'm damn happy to have such a big, wonderful family that wants to help us celebrate."

"Come down here, lads," Ryan called to us from just below the wall we still stood on.

"Just so you know. I don't need a big ceremony, but I'm thrilled to be doing this here. It really feels right," I said, and kissed his hand before we both made our way back down the winding staircase to the bottom.

Twenty-Three
Rings

LANCE

I wasn't sure what came over me at the castle. But whatever it was, I was glad it had happened. There was never going to be someone else who meant more to me and getting married here with my new family and both our families from home felt more than right.

"You two are getting married, are ye?" Ryan asked as we walked to the car. We'd invited Gerald to go to lunch, but since he was still working, he wasn't able to.

"Yes, and we'd love for you and Gerald to go," Billie said, his smile still as bright as it had been since I'd proposed.

Ryan smiled as he slid into the back seat. "I'll ask him."

"Okay then," I said over the top of the car to Billie, who stifled a laugh.

"Are we ready to go back to Castlecomer?" I asked after getting in the car and looked in the rearview mirror.

"Let's go to lunch somewhere close," Billie said.

We found a pub nearby and were seated immediately. "I'm going to miss the pub food," I said and looked at the menu.

"Me too," Billie said.

Ryan sat quietly, looking at the menu, an amused expression on his face, before setting it down and folding his hands on top of it.

"Everyone ready to order?" the bartender asked.

We placed our orders and sat sipping our drinks. "This was a great day," Billie said.

"Ryan, do you mind if we go to a jewelry store on the way back?"

"No, Lance, I was waiting for one of you to ask. I can recommend one if you'd like," he chuckled.

"I'll owe you one. I wanted to ask you at the castle, but I wasn't sure you'd want to go. We talked and we want to get traditional Irish rings. Or something that will remind us of Ireland. I'm not sure there even is a traditional wedding ring."

"There's plenty that should match your needs," Ryan said.

"Perfect. I never want to forget that this is where we got married," Billie said.

"Were you able to change your hotel and airline reservations?" Ryan asked just as our food arrived.

"Yes, it must have been meant to be. Apparently, the hotel was mostly empty for next week, and we'd paid for airline tickets we could cancel or change." It was one more thing falling into place, and proving all this was meant to happen as it had.

"There's a jewelry store near here that I think might have what you're looking for," Ryan said with a grin.

We finished eating one more delicious pub meal, and after paying, followed Ryan's directions. The streets narrowed as we went to a part of town that was a combination of houses and businesses. He pointed to what had to be the narrowest building I'd ever seen and a sign that read Rosie's Rings.

"This is owned by a good friend of mine," Ryan said, and led the way.

We walked into a jewelry store that felt even smaller on the inside than it looked from the outside. Instead of a bunch of display cases, there was one counter at the back of the store, which we followed Ryan to. He tapped on a bell that was set there and the three of us waited.

A woman about his age walked out from the back of the store and her eyes lit up as soon as she saw Ryan.

"Oh, Ryan, how are ye?" she asked and came around the counter to give him a hug.

"I'm good, Rose. How are you?"

"I can't complain," she said, before looking at the two of us. "Who'd you bring with you, Ryan?"

"This is my great-nephew Lance, and his fiancé Billie. They'd like to buy some rings."

"Well congratulations. Now, what kind of rings are you looking for?" she asked, right down to business.

"We both like white gold and platinum. Simple bands with an Irish design. But we're not sure what that looks like exactly," I explained while Billie took my hand and squeezed it.

"There're a few options. Some go with the Claddagh design, but I like the simpler, more classic models. The Celtic Knot is my favorite. Let me show you." She walked to the backroom and came back out with several trays, each holding a variety of rings. Billie and I immediately got busy narrowing down what we liked and what was not us.

Some were too thin, and others were way too thick and chunky. But we found a few that we both loved. Seeing Billie with a ring on his finger did strange things to me. I never thought of myself as someone who would want to get married, but now that was all that was on my mind. It was a relief to know we wouldn't need to wait because if this had turned into a long engagement; I wasn't sure I'd survive.

"How about this one?" Billie asked, bringing me back to the whole reason we were here.

It was smooth and plain on the outside, but then he pointed out the inside. Hidden on the inner surface was a beautiful carving. "It's a hidden Celtic Knot," Rose explained. "It's made of platinum."

It was too small for me, but I put it as far down my finger as it would go, and Billie gasped. "Lance, it's the one," he said. I met his eyes, and he gripped my arm while tracing his finger along the smooth outer surface of the ring.

"I agree. We won't find one more perfect."

Billie leaned in and kissed me before we both turned to Rose. "We'll take this one, and we'll need two," Billie said and held up two fingers.

Rose smiled, and Ryan laughed at our antics. "I can have them sized and ready by tomorrow. How does that work for you?"

"That's perfect, thank you so much," I said. She double-checked our ring sizes and took down our information. After paying, the three of us were on the road again.

"Thanks, Ryan, I'm pretty sure we would have never found the perfect ring if you weren't with us," Billie said.

"Just glad I could help you," Ryan said. I looked at him in the rearview mirror as he grinned all the way back to his door, and once again, I thanked Billie for making this trip happen.

Twenty-Four

The Announcement

BILLIE

I held Lance's hand for the drive back to the hotel, unable to be near him without touching him. He glanced at me and smiled, and I knew he felt the same way. "What an amazing day," I said.

"It was. I don't know what made me decide to propose in that moment, but I'm glad I didn't ignore the opportunity."

"I second that! And how fortunate was it that Ryan knew of that cool jewelry store? I can't wait to get our rings. They're so perfect. Thanks again Ryan." He nodded his head in reply and focused on the landscape we drove by.

"You're so perfect. Thank you for making every dream I've ever had come true. I can't wait to put a ring on that finger, so the whole world knows how much I love you," Lance whispered.

"Aww," I swooned. "Don't make me cry. If I get started, I'll never stop." I acted like I was joking, but the truth was every time he spoke to me like that, my stomach fluttered, and it had nothing to do with being hungry. He made me feel emotions I never thought were possible to feel.

"I love you, and we're going straight to Joseph's." Ryan chuckled and shook his head but remained silent.

"As if I expected anything else?" I knew without a doubt he couldn't wait to tell his new family. It was exciting sharing the news with his family and mine, but they had been expecting it for a while. Joseph and his family had no idea how long we'd talked about getting married and were just so happy to meet us that this seemed like news they'd really enjoy. We drove across the little bridge into Castlecomer. But instead of turning into the parking lot for the hotel, Lance continued down the street before parking right in front of the café. "What are you doing?" I laughed.

"Making an entrance?" He shrugged and took my hand as soon as we were both out of the car. Ryan got out and walked behind us to the door.

"Hey, Lance, how was the castle?" Joseph called from the kitchen.

"It was great." Lance looked around at the patrons, who were currently eating a late lunch. Most of them didn't pay us any attention, but a few had looked up when Joseph had greeted him. "We got engaged. We're going to get married here. This week. So, what do you think, Joseph, can you plan a wedding in a few days?"

The entire café went silent, and a few people looked from Lance to Joseph before he tore his apron off and rushed over to pick each of us up in a big hug and spin us around. "Are you serious? You better be serious. If you're not, I'll make you pay for it," he threatened, but his bright smile gave away his happiness. He clapped Ryan on the back and pulled him in for a side-hug. Ryan shook his head and laughed and looked like the weight of the world had been lifted from his shoulders.

"We're having a wedding?" a woman seated at one of the tables asked. I didn't know her, but her face was full of expectation, like she was waiting to be invited.

Joseph turned to face the diners. "Folks, we're having a wedding, and you're all invited." He clapped his hands, and everyone cheered and toasted us with whatever they were drinking.

"I'll leave you to it," Ryan said as he walked out the door with a wave.

"Come on, lads, tell me all about what you have planned." He guided us back into the kitchen and hugged both of us again. "Well?"

"So, we were thinking we could use the park behind the café. Do you think that would be possible?" Lance asked.

"Give me a second," Joseph said, and tapped out a message on his phone. A chime sounded almost as soon as he pressed send. He read the message before mumbling to himself. "Fucking arse." He smirked and sent another message, and just like before, a reply came almost immediately.

Lance and I looked at each other with wide eyes. Everything about this was happening so differently than I could have ever imagined, and I loved it. I laughed, and Lance pulled me into a hug with a kiss to the side of my head.

"Right, boys, we're all set. We can use the area with the stage and tables on the far side under the trees. It's beautiful. We'll get the family on it and start decorating tomorrow. Don't you two worry, we'll get it all ready."

"We can't let you do it all," I said.

"Ye can and ya will."

"Okay then. Do you know someone who could perform the service?" Lance asked.

"Of course, I do. Didn't Ryan tell you? He's married many happy couples. He probably told you all about how much he loves old shit, but he's also been officiating weddings for years."

"Lance, it's perfect," I said, and I couldn't believe it was real. Everything was falling into place so perfectly.

"Are the American relatives going to join us?" Joseph asked.

"Yes, both families. They're going to get here as soon as they can arrange it. Most will probably get here midweek," I said.

"That's perfect. Let me make a few phone calls and get it all arranged. What kind of food are you thinking?" Joseph had taken out a pad of paper and took notes as he spoke.

"We want to do a very traditional Irish wedding. Since this is Lance's heritage, we want to celebrate it and make Ireland a big part of our ceremony," I said. Joseph stopped writing and locked eyes with me.

"You know you two are killing me with all the feelings, right?" he said, before leaning over the top of the table and hugging us both again. "It's been a genuine pleasure getting to know you."

"Do you know where we can rent tuxedos?" Lance asked as soon as Joseph released us again.

"Lance, you know we're related to half of the county. Of course, I know someone. Now, how many are you thinking will attend the wedding?" He held his pen ready to write more notes.

"We're not sure. I mean, we know how many will be here on our side, but we have no clue how many of the locals will be there," I said, and grinned at Joseph.

"Well, looks like we'll need a lot of food then, and a cake. A beautiful cake. I'm going to call Mum. She'll kill me if I don't let her bake it." Joseph was off and running. Adding more to his list while taking care of customers. And inviting each and every one of them.

"You realize the small wedding we always talked about is not going to be small at all," I whispered to Lance.

"I know, and I can't wait."

Twenty-Five
Tuxes and Kilts

Lance

The next day was spent trying to book our families' flights here and making a plan to pick them up. With my mom, my siblings, and their significant others, and then with all of Billie's family, there were a lot of us. We were sitting at the hotel, both of us online, trying to figure out how to get everyone here in time.

"Billie, take a break," I said, when I noticed he was about to pull a chunk of hair out of the top of his head.

"I can't. I want to get it all done so I can focus on the wedding, not flights."

I gently untangled his hand from his hair and kissed it before taking it in mine. "Let's do this. We'll find a ride service that will bring them here. We already have the hotel, so we don't need to worry about that. But I think they're going to need to get flights for themselves. It's just too complicated, and with the time zone difference, it's hard to speak with them. Give them some links to flights you find and let them work it out."

"I'm sorry. I was hoping this would be easier than getting married at home, but it seems like it's almost worse."

"Baby, all that matters to me is that you show up at the end of the aisle. I love you, and while I love the idea of getting married here, I'd be just as happy to get married at a courthouse, or wherever you get married in Ireland."

He smiled then, and my chest eased in relief, and I took a deep breath. "I love you," he whispered.

"I know. Now let's get that information and send them all an email. Then I really want to go look at tuxes."

His eyes lit up at that. "Well, that sounds way more fun than looking at flights. Give me thirty minutes and I'll be ready to go." His fingers flew over the keys and true to his word, in thirty minutes we were walking out the door.

"I have the information. It's close," I rambled. "I'm so ready for this. We have the perfect rings, now we just need to find the perfect tux. What style did you want to try on?" We walked to the car, and he grinned the whole way.

"How about we wear kilts? They're traditional, and I know you wanted to have a very Irish wedding. So? What do you think?"

"I think I can't wait to see you in one."

We followed Joseph's directions down a few narrow streets until we came to a small shop that had tuxedos and other formal wear on display in the window. I stopped and looked at one in particular. It was a black jacket accented with silver buttons down the front and on each cuff, over a black vest with matching buttons. A kilt was worn instead of pants, and heavy woolen socks with black dress shoes. "It's perfect."

"I can imagine you in it. Come on, let's go see," Billie said and dragged me out of my daydream and into the shop.

"Hello, gentlemen, something I can help you with?" the shopkeeper, a man who looked to be in his seventies with a big moustache, and not much hair on his head, asked.

"Yes, Joseph sent us here, he—" I started.

"Oh, you're the Yanks, well, come on then. I've got a few selections ready for you. Let me just take a few measurements." He whipped a tape measure off his neck like it was some sort of weapon, and before Billie or I could say a word, we'd been shoved into separate changing rooms to try on a suit he'd put in there.

"The name's Ian, by the way. Joseph told me to expect you today, and that you'd be looking for some traditional wedding garb. We're always happy to help anyone related to Joseph," he said as he stood just outside the dressing rooms.

I looked at the clothes he'd hung up for me, and while I knew what to do with the dress shirt, vest, and jacket, I had no clue how to put a kilt on.

"I don't know what to put on first," Billie called from the room he was in.

"Okay, lads, it's best to start with your shirt," Ian directed. "Next you'll put on your hose."

"Did you say hose?" I asked.

"What does he mean hose?" Billie asked.

"Your socks, pull on your socks," Ian bellowed. "Pull them all the way up, then you'll attach your flashes."

"What the—?" Billie muttered, and I looked at the items hanging there and had no clue what he meant.

"The garters, lads, you'll want to attach them to the top of your socks just below the knee. There're two flags there too, those go on the garters and after you fold the top edge of the socks down, those will show."

I did as he said, and since I had no clue how it was supposed to look, I hoped I had it right.

"What size shoe are ye?" Ian asked, and after we answered, he walked away mumbling something about stupid Yank shoe measurements.

I poked my head out of the dressing room just as Billie did the same. "Hey," he said.

"Hey, what do you think so far?"

"I'm glad Ian's telling me what goes where, or I'd be lost. I'd probably have used the flags for a pocket square," he said, and grinned.

"Okay, here you go. Just put them on the best you can. We'll worry about lacing them later."

The laces were extra-long, and the shoes were made different from anything I'd worn before. The socks showed through the laces on top of the shoes, but no way was I questioning what Ian had going on.

"Now you'll want to take your kilt off the hanger. Open it up and hold it behind you, making sure your shirt is smooth under it. Take the strap in your right hand and thread it through the slit by your left hip. Pull it through and strap it to the buckle that's right there. Then you'll wrap the other side over to the back of your right hip. There're two buckles there. Use the top one first and you'll want it to be comfortable, not too tight, but not too loose. The bottom buckle is mostly decorative. Let me know when you've got it."

I held up the long swath of fabric and tried to do what he said, but while it sounded simple, it was anything but. I tried it one way, and it was obviously the wrong way, then I tried another, and by then I'd forgotten his directions.

"I'm gonna need some help," I said and stuck my head out the door just as Billie's head also appeared.

"Me too. Sorry, Ian, but kilts are hard," he said, making Ian laugh.

"Okay, lads, step outside your room and bring your kilt," he said, and grumbled something else under his breath that I'm pretty sure was an Irish curse, but I smiled and gladly accepted his help.

Twenty-Six

Grooms

BILLIE

Ian patiently helped both of us with our kilts before showing us where all the accessories went. When he finally stepped back from Lance, I turned to face him. He took my breath away. He stood there looking as regal and traditional as any proper Irishman would on his wedding day.

"Wow," I breathed out, making Ian laugh.

"You two clean up quite nicely," he said. "Now, we could get your family crest for the plaid brooch. There's a shop nearby that carries nearly all the traditional names."

Lance still hadn't looked away from me. His eyes trailed over every little detail from my shoes to the broach Ian had just mentioned. "You look so different," he murmured before stepping forward and running his hand along the collar of the dress jacket.

"So do you. But I like it." I smiled and signaled for him to turn around. Yep, he looked just as good from every angle.

"I can't believe we're doing this," he said as Ian fussed over every little detail, making sure it all fit as it was supposed to.

"Stand here next to each other. Let's see how you look together," Ian said.

He stood us side by side in front of a full-length mirror. "Oh wow," I said, and put my arm through Lance's. "We do look pretty good."

"Yes, you do. Like two proper grooms." Ian stood back like the proud man he was and continued to critique every minor detail. "They'll need to be tailored slightly, but it won't take more than a day. Which should be perfect timing for your wedding."

"That sounds wonderful," Lance said, and once again met my eyes with a smile. "Could you take a picture of us?"

"Of course." Ian took his phone and snapped several photos. Some together and some of us individually. When it came time to change, we were both hesitant, and not just because it was a lot of work to take it all back off. For me, it was because wearing these clothes pushed me one step closer to marrying the man I love. "I'll just go and write everything up," Ian said, then took his tape measure and the pad of paper he'd been taking notes on and left us.

"You really look handsome," I said, and held Lance's hands out while I took him in.

"You do too, and I really can't wait to marry you."

"We'd better hurry and change before Ian comes looking for us," I said and looked toward the door he'd left through.

"One thing first," Lance said, and pulled me to him. He kissed me, and it was familiar yet somehow more filled with feeling than any kiss before. I wondered if this was what it was like when you knew you were marrying the perfect person, or if it was just how it was between the two of us. Not that it mattered. One way or another, we were getting married.

We forced ourselves back into the dressing rooms and slowly figured out how to take everything off. It was a *little* easier coming off than it had been going on, but it still took a few minutes. When we were done, we walked out to find Ian hunched over the front desk.

"Okay, boys, I have your information and we'll have a final fitting soon. I plan to be at the hotel in plenty of time to get the two of you dressed properly, and I'll be at the wedding, so if you need any help, just have someone come and find me."

"You're going?" Lance asked.

"Well, of course, you're my great-nephew twice removed," Ian said, and crossed his arms.

"You're what?" Lance's eyes widened as he listened.

"I don't understand it either, but that's what my auntie said, and I believe her. She's always been good with who is related and how."

"Wow, Joseph wasn't kidding when he said we were all related." Lance smiled then and pulled me close.

"Nope, and soon we'll have even more family." He tilted his head toward me and I loved the fact I was included in their family.

We walked out to the car just as my phone alerted with a message. "Looks like my family has all gotten their airline tickets. They hope to be here late the day after tomorrow." I breathed a sigh of relief, after all the times they'd said they'd come visit and hadn't, I'd been holding my breath waiting for them to cancel.

"They'll be here just in time. Good thing we weren't planning on eloping," Lance said.

"Have you heard from your mom or anyone?"

"Yes, they were waiting to buy tickets for the kids, but the adults are all accounted for. They want to see if they can have the kids stay with friends until they get back."

"Oh good, it sounds like it really is coming together."

"It certainly is. I still can't believe it."

"You have an amazing family." Whether he knew it or not, they were all cut from the same cloth, and all of them were as hardworking and determined as he was. My family was the same, but different. My family were more the throw them out there and hope they survive types. Lance had been trained and guided through his career by a mother who knew exactly what she was doing. "Did you want anyone else to walk in the wedding?" I asked.

"I hadn't thought about it, but I'd like my mom to give me away. Maybe your mom and dad could do the same?"

"I like that idea. And my sister will kill me if I don't let her in."

"She could be one of the attendants. Maybe one of my sisters could do that too." Lance and I chatted about who we'd ask, and who we wouldn't. "What about Joseph? I feel like he should be involved too. He's done so much."

"Do you think he'd mind since he insisted on doing the food?"

"Only one way to find out. Maybe he could be the ring bearer?" I suggested and imagined Joseph holding a tiny satin pillow with the rings cradled on it.

"Oh, that might be good. I'm going to ask him."

"Lance, I was joking. I'm sure he'd rather not."

Lance pulled over in front of a pub and tapped out a message. "Let's get some food. All this trying on clothes has got me starving."

We'd just stepped out of the car when his phone sounded with a message. He laughed as he read it. "You know I'd love to be the ring bearer, or the flower girl. You name it, Lance, and I'll be there for you and Billie."

"Well, I guess it's settled then." I took Lance's hand as we walked inside. "Our small wedding is going to be fairly big after all." Lance squeezed my hand and grinned, and I knew for sure that didn't bother him, not one little bit.

"We'll need to have everyone call Ian. They'll all need kilts," he said as we slid into a booth.

"Yes, they will." As I looked over the menu, I imagined Lance dressed in his wedding attire, surrounded by our family, all dressed in Irish garb, and I could hardly wait for the day to come.

Twenty-Seven
Last Minute Details

LANCE

The relatives had started to roll in. First it was Billie's sister, Bex, then one of my nephews. His parents had arrived late last night, and my mom was due sometime today. So far, they were all still sleeping at the hotel, and I couldn't say I blamed them. It was a long flight and very last minute, so I was just happy they'd been able to make it happen.

"We're going to go prep with Joseph today, right?" Billie asked. We were relaxing in our room. It was one of the few times we'd taken time to just kick back and not be running around all over Ireland.

"Yes, he said he doesn't need help, but I call bullshit. We have no clue how many are showing up and I'd rather have too much food than not enough." I'd made a list of a few dishes I thought would be good, but I really wanted to keep the menu regional and traditional to Ireland. Billie and I had googled what that meant, but after we'd gotten so many varied answers, we decided we'd leave the menu to Joseph.

"I could go for a coffee," Billie said and stretched, showing off a hint of that toned stomach I loved to touch.

"Let's go to the little place by the market." There were so many small businesses close to us. It made it very easy to get whatever we needed.

"Sounds good, quick and easy." Billie kissed my cheek as he opened the door to our room.

The fresh air felt great after spending the morning indoors. It was beautiful weather, and I was again reminded how perfect this week was turning out. We walked to the market and, after buying coffee and a piece of lemon slice for each of us, we stood outside. "Why don't we walk over to the park and get a better idea of where everything will be," I said, and pointed in the general direction.

"I can't believe we didn't think of that before. Let's go." Billie headed in the direction I'd indicated, toward the park behind Joseph's café. We hadn't explored this area next to the small river that the bridge went over and was actually close to a very large, wooded area.

"This is a lot bigger than I thought it was," I said, and the two of us walked along the many paths we found there. It was divided into several areas, but when we came to a clearing surrounded by trees, I knew this was where the wedding would be held.

I took Billie's hand in mine as we walked into the center of the clearing. He set his coffee cup down and took mine from me before holding both my hands in his. "This is where I'll marry the only man I'll ever love." His eyes were full of sincerity, and his voice held no humor. He meant every word.

"I'm the luckiest man in the whole damn world." My throat was tight with emotions that shocked me, and I blamed it on the fact we were really getting married, and our families were either already here or on their way.

"Well, one of them."

"I can't wait to marry you, Mr. Watts," I whispered.

"I can't wait to marry *you*, Mr. Karl."

"Mr. and Mr. Karl."

We both spun around to find Bex, Billie's sister, walking toward us. "Bex!" Billie said and spun her around. "I thought you'd still be sleeping."

"I woke up and showered and couldn't stand to be in my room another second. The guy at the front desk said he'd seen you walking this way, so I thought I'd take a chance. How are you doing, Lance?" She hugged me the same as she did Billie.

"I'm doing great. Thank you so much for making the trip on such short notice."

"Are you kidding? Any excuse to take a trip to Ireland. So, what do you need help with?" Billie and I filled her in on all we'd completed and what was still needing to be done.

"We wanted to ask you something." Billie squeezed my hand while he met her eyes.

"What is it? Is everything okay?" She looked between the two of us as she waited for an answer.

"Everything is perfect. Would you stand up with us when we get married? Lance and I want you and Rob to be in the wedding. He's going to ask his sister and her son to stand up for him." Billie grinned at her while he spoke. This was what he wanted, to have our families not only here to watch us get married, but to stand up with us.

"Are you guys sure? I never expected to be included in the ceremony."

"We're more than sure," I said.

"I'd love to be, and I'm sure Rob will feel the same. He's getting here later tonight. Thank you so much for including us in your special day." Her eyes were a little teary, and I looked away and cleared my throat. "It's going to be a beautiful ceremony."

"Wait until you see all we have planned. Which reminds me, we'll need to call Ian to get everyone else fitted with their wedding attire," Billie said.

"Wedding attire?" Bex repeated.

"We're going traditional. Don't worry, you'll love it. We spoke to Ian, and he said he'd have everything we need, and if he doesn't have it, he can get it," I explained as we walked toward the hotel.

"You have to meet Joseph. He's Lance's uncle. He owns the cutest little café, and he's the best. Everything he cooks tastes great. He's going to do all the food for the wedding," Billie said.

"Does he need help?" Bex asked.

"He'll say he doesn't, but I want him to enjoy the wedding and not be working all day. We were going to help prep today."

"Lance, I knew your family was a perfect match for ours." Bex took Billie's arm, and the three of us walked back toward the cafe.

"We are all definitely worker bees." It was true. Both of our families worked hard and loved it. Billie and I met over work, and now we'd make a lifetime promise to love each other over a chance meeting at my food truck.

"Well, this worker bee needs a coffee." Bex walked to the cafe and the two of us stood there for a moment before Billie turned to me.

"We need to call Ian," he said, and took out his phone.

"Hopefully he knows where he can get dresses for the moms and Bex," I mumbled, and Billie laughed.

"Everything else has worked out, so I have complete faith this will too. Ian, hey, this is Billie Watts."

"What are you needing now?" he yelled, so loud Billie didn't need the speaker on.

"Are you able to get us dresses—"

"I've already made arrangements. Don't worry, we just need the girls to try them on. It's all been taken care of."

"You're the best, Ian," he said, and smiled at Billie.

"That I am, and I'll see you boys in two hours for your final fitting." He hung up without another word.

"Well, guess we better go talk to Joseph now, or we won't get another chance."

"It's coming together, baby," Billie said, and all I could do was smile and imagine how handsome he'd look when we were standing in the park surrounded by our family on our wedding day.

Twenty-Eight

All Together

Billie

The families were officially all here. "I'm pretty sure the hotel is regretting letting us have the whole place," Lance mumbled as we walked past the lobby and outside. The normally quiet area was now filled with the sounds of voices and laughter.

"Nah, they don't mind," I said and took his hand. "Come on, today is the day we prep for the wedding. Are you ready for this?"

"Oh, I've been ready. I just keep thinking how much easier it would have been to elope."

"Lance, I know you don't mean that." Our plans were all last minute, but it was coming together. The fact most of our family had flown here was amazing and no small miracle.

"No, I don't." He pulled me to him and rested his forehead against mine. "I can't wait to marry you. It's just a little overwhelming right now."

I grinned at him. My soon-to-be husband, who could handle a lunch rush with no problem, was going crazy trying to round up everyone and make sure they were all doing everything the way he wanted it. Even if he wasn't really sure how he wanted it. "We'll go see what Joseph has going on, then we'll leave for Ian's from there. They're both as bad as you are at wanting to control it all, so don't worry, baby, it's all going to be perfect."

"Oh god you realize Joseph's going to be butting heads with Mom?" Lance pulled back enough to meet my eyes. "We need to get to the café." He grabbed my hand and practically dragged me along until we were at the door.

"This doesn't look good," I said as we both peered inside. Joseph and Lance's mom, Alice, were both standing at the front of the restaurant and looked to be organizing everyone for what needed to be done.

Lance pushed the door open and walked over to the two of them. "What's going on?"

"Well, good morning, you two. Joseph and I are just organizing everyone. He has the menu all figured out, so we just need to get everything prepped for tomorrow." Alice led us to where a group was seated at one table chopping various ingredients. Another group was busy with preparing a few different meats for roasting, another was preparing side dishes. Then, on the bakery side of the café, a few people were preparing to bake a variety of sweet treats and what looked like some sourdough rolls.

"Are you making fresh sourdough for the wedding?" Lance asked.

"Yes, it's what you came here to share with me so it's only right we bake it. We're also going to make some small sliders out of your lobster recipe," Joseph said. "I paid attention when you made it. Hopefully, I can duplicate it. There's not a chance we wouldn't be serving those at your wedding." He set his hands on his hips and looked around his café. It was obvious the chaos was where he thrived.

Lance walked over and hugged him. "Thank you so much. You can't imagine how much that means to me. It's the food that brought us together." He smiled at me, and my heart clenched. It was all going to happen. Soon, we'd be married.

Lance tipped his head, and his eyes softened. "Don't start or you'll get me crying."

"I'm trying not to, but I really can't believe this is all happening." Bex waved a big spoon at me from the side dish area, and my dad grinned at me from the meat area.

"Want to know what's on the menu?" Joseph asked, thankfully changing the subject.

"Of course, we do," I said.

"For starters, we'll have smoked salmon on soda bread, lamb lollipops and shots of leek soup," Joseph read from a piece of paper that looked like it was splattered with most of what was on the list.

"How big are the shots of leek soup?" Lance asked.

Joseph showed him the small bowls that were the perfect size for a small, single serving. "Perfect, what's next?"

"We'll have a lovely green salad with a variety of different vegetables on it, and a balsamic vinaigrette. We're only doing one dressing. I'm not messing with thirty different choices, so if anyone wants ranch dressing, they can bring their own."

"Noted," Lance said and tried to sneak a peek at the entrees.

"Patience, lad, for the entrées we'll have salmon en croute, herb roasted chicken, roasted beef, and meat pies. Mum is making the cake; oh, it'll be a grand one." He read down his list again and looked between the two of us. "Well? What do you think?"

Lance put his hands on his hips and matched Joseph's stance. "What sides do you have planned?"

Joseph rattled off the list, and Lance smiled. "You're sure we can have all that ready for tomorrow?"

"Hey, he's worried we won't be ready," Joseph said to the room. At first everyone was silent, but then a loud grumble spread through the room.

"We'll have it ready, Lance, now make yourself useful and get busy on the rolls for the lobster," Alice said from across the room where she and Annie were busy mixing up something in the bakery area.

"Looks like we're in for a long day," I said, as I joined him next to the counter we'd used the other night.

"I wouldn't want it any other way. It's in our blood," Lance said, and kissed my cheek.

"That it is, lad, now get busy. I need you to make soda bread too," Joseph said, and walked off to yell at another relative that they weren't working fast enough. Lance laughed, and the two of us settled in for a long ass day and I knew without question, both of us loved it.

"This is our family," Lance whispered and looked around the room. Some faces were familiar, and some were brand new, but all were pitching in to help us, and we appreciated them all.

"Yes, and after tomorrow our family will grow even more," Joseph said, and looked between the two of us like a proud father.

"Joseph, get to work," Annie yelled from the bakery.

"Okay, lads, playtime is over." He handed us both an apron, and we celebrated the night before the wedding by cooking until the wee hours of the morning. It was perfect.

Twenty-Nine

Wedding Day

LANCE

I rolled over and buried my face in the nape of Billie's neck. I wanted to remember every scent and experience of this day, starting with waking up next to the man I love. Today we'd become one, and I couldn't wait.

"Good morning, future husband," Billie whispered. It was still early, and I hadn't realized he was also awake.

"Good morning. Are you ready for today?" Throwing my leg over his and snuggling even closer than I was, I breathed him in.

"So ready." He rolled over to face me. "I've been hoping for this day since the first day we met." His lips met mine and I would have been more than happy to spend the day in bed, but not today.

It was still early, and the wedding didn't start until three, but we still had a few things to take care of. The wedding party went to Ian's shop yesterday afternoon. Since he was an expert in efficiency, he had everyone fitted and ready to go in a couple of hours.

Bex, my sisters, my mom, and Billie's mom had gone to the dress shop to pick up their dresses. I had nothing to do with picking them out, so I hoped whatever they ended up with was something they all were happy with.

"What are you thinking about?" Billie asked.

"The dresses." I smiled, and he smiled back, so big and bright I couldn't resist kissing him. "Hopefully they like them."

"They do. Bex said they're beautiful."

"Oh, thank god. I don't think I could deal with one more errand." We'd spent nearly all-day prepping and getting any supplies that could not be delivered.

"Don't worry, if there's anything we forgot, we don't need it."

We spent the morning holed up in our room. Both of us knew once we left, we'd be dealing with wedding details, and neither of us was ready for that yet. After ordering breakfast and showering separately, we walked out the door to our room and straight into Bex.

"Where have you two been? We've been calling and messaging. It's going to be time soon, and Joseph wants you to taste everything before he's willing to sign off on it. His words, not mine."

"We're on our way there now," Billie said, and the three of us hurried over to the café.

"Guys, you need to approve it all. I know you saw most of it yesterday, but I want your blessing," Joseph said. He'd made up sampling trays and for the next hour, the two of us tried everything he put out.

"It's all delicious. Don't change a thing," I said, and Joseph laughed.

"Oh, this is what you're getting. Just making sure it was edible." I turned to face him with a mouth full of food. "I'm just kidding you," he said, then laughed.

"Where's everyone at?" Billie asked before laughing at my expression.

"They're all at the park decorating. Now, I know they don't want you to see it before it's all done so why don't you help me portion and package everything so we're ready to go? It's only a few hours now." Joseph seemed to know just what I'd need to keep my mind from racing through all the details I hoped were not forgotten.

Just like he'd promised, Ian arrived at the hotel with two men in tow to help with the kilts and all the accessories. The hotel let us use one of their small conference rooms so we could all get ready together. Billie's dad stood in front of the mirror while Ian helped him dress in his kilt.

"What do you think, Dad?" Billie asked and stepped up next to him.

"I like it, and I can't wait to see you two dressed." He looked so proud as he looked between us, and I hoped Billie could see it the way I did. He deserved to know how his dad felt.

"Speaking of," Ian said with a stern look at both of us. "It's time for the grooms to get dressed. Now, if everyone else could go do whatever you need to do, I'd appreciate it." They all grumbled, but another stern look from Ian and they were gone. "Now, I'll need one of you to go into that room because you're not to see each other again until you're walking down that aisle."

"But why do we need to do that?" I asked.

"Because you need some tradition. Even if you don't in-clude them all, it's okay to add some," Ian said like he said this at least twenty times a day.

"Go on, Lance. I'll stay here, and we'll meet later at the top of the aisle," Billie said before he kissed me and walked over to where his suit was hung.

Ian led me to another small room next door and immedi-ately got to work, telling me what to do and where to stand.

When he finished, he stood next to me and gave me a critical look. "You look like a proper Irishman. You and your guy are going to make a handsome couple."

"Thanks, Ian. We couldn't have done this without your help."

"I know. Now go out there and make the family proud." He gathered his things and tipped his head at one of the guys who'd come with him and helped him carry the bags that had held our suits. As they walked out, Mom walked in.

"Are you ready for this?" she asked. She was beautiful, dressed in a deep green dress that was shorter in the front and draped long in the back. Her hair was pulled up on her head and held in place by a row of pins. One of them had a small scrap of what I now knew was the family tartan, the same that decorated the edge of my socks.

"Yeah. I still can't believe it's happening." I tried not to think too hard about it for fear of letting my nerves get the best of me.

"It is. I'm so proud of both of you. You and Billie found your match made in heaven." I didn't miss it when her voice cracked slightly, even through her smile. "Now, we'd better go before Joseph sends someone to look for us."

She looped her arm through mine, and we walked down the hall that led to the front of the hotel. There were a few people sitting in the lobby, but my focus was on the park across the street that I could see through the glass doors. Blue and green streamers hung from the trees and the tops of poles that had been placed near the rows of chairs to hang lights from. It was still light out, but I could easily see the large glass bulbs that would provide light when the sun set. People were already gathering there, but I couldn't make out who. I looked around for Billie but didn't see him.

A small carriage pulled up in front of the hotel, and the driver looked over at us and grinned. "Liam?" The young guy from Joseph's restaurant straightened at the mention of his name and tipped his head.

"Aye, Joseph said to hitch up Nellie and give you a ride to the wedding in style. So here we are." The horse threw her head like she understood every word he said. He waited patiently for the two of us to get into the seat behind where he sat, and with a click of his tongue, we were off. The horse followed along the path we'd walked on that led to the park.

"Are you giving Billie a ride, too?" I asked. We turned to go into the park and in the distance, I could see people were already seated, and tables had been set up under the trees. It was beautiful, and as Liam pulled the buggy up to the end of the aisle, I saw Billie standing there. His legs were just visible under his kilt as he stood with his hands folded in front of him.

He walked over and held his hand out to steady me as I stepped down. His brother stepped forward and helped Mom down, but my focus was completely on Billie. "Hey," I said, and wondered why I felt so shy around a man who knew me better than anyone.

"Hey, ready to get married?" His eyes sparkled, and his smile was bright as he gripped my hand.

"So, ready." I knew I shouldn't kiss him, but I leaned in, and he leaned back.

"Your mom already threatened me about this. No kissing until you put a ring on it. Her words, not mine."

"I love you." He grinned and squeezed my hand as he led me to the top of the aisle.

Thirty

Mr. and Mr.

BILLIE

Lance and I stood side by side at the aisle with our friends and family seated in front of us. We'd changed our minds about having our parents escort us, and decided we wanted to walk together. They were lined up in front of us smiling, while they waited for us. I forced myself not to look at Bex or I knew I'd have a hard time keeping it together.

The music started, and I noticed Joseph was standing at the front by Ryan, playing a set of bagpipes. "I did not expect that," I mumbled, making Lance cough to cover his laugh.

We walked slowly toward the front, taking the time to greet each person, and say hello to family we hadn't met yet. There were so many people I'd never seen before, but they all acknowledged us like we were old friends.

When I finally looked to the end of the aisle again, everyone who was a part of the wedding were standing there watching us slowly make our way to them. Dad smiled and I had to control myself from choking up even more than I already was. It was surreal. We were getting married, and all of our family was here. All the hurt feelings from the past faded away, none of it mattered. They were here for us when we needed them the most.

Lance reached for my hand and squeezed it seeming to know I needed him then. His eyes met mine and instantly it was just us. We were in the bubble we found ourselves in when we were alone at the apartment spending a lazy Sunday morning in bed. I loved him, and he loved me, and that love grew and grew with every moment we spent together.

"Well, gentlemen, are you ready?" Ryan asked when we stood directly in front of him. He was dressed slightly differently than the rest of us, including Joseph. His kilt looked more official somehow, and more authentic. Then I remembered how invested he was in history and imagined it was probably very old and had a million stories that went along with it.

"We are," Lance said, bringing me back to attention.

"Yes, we definitely are."

He grinned at us and started to recite what he had written inside a small notebook he held in front of him. "We are gathered here today to bless the marriage of Lance Karl and William Watts," he began, his accent even heavier as he read the words of the customary Irish vows we'd all agreed on. Mostly because it talked about sharing food, and for Lance and me, there couldn't have been more perfect words.

We held hands as we stood facing each other, and I could feel love radiating from Lance as we took turns saying our parts. Neither of us were big on public speaking, so we stuck to the program and didn't write our own vows. Besides, we always told each other exactly how we felt with nothing held back.

"I give you my heart, and pledge you my love," Lance repeated after Ryan as he slid the ring on my finger, and I repeated those same words back to him.

Ryan took out a length of silver ribbon and wrapped it around our hands before tying a neat bow. "I bind you both together, and as God as my witness, let no man tear apart what the good lord has seen fit to join. I pronounce you married, go ahead and kiss your husband." He smiled and Lance reached for me with his free hand and kissed me. His tongue glided against mine, and even though we'd kissed plenty of times, my heart stuttered.

"I love you," he whispered against my lips.

"As I love you."

"May I present to you Mr. and Mr. Karl," Ryan said and clapped each of us on the shoulder as we turned to face our family. Our hands were still bound together, but neither of us were in a hurry to have a breath of space between us. Joseph started playing the pipes again, and the two of us started to walk back down the aisle. Mom pulled me in for a hug before I got too far away, followed by Dad and Bex. Lance was busy with relatives we'd met while we were here, and they were introducing him to others he'd yet to meet.

"Congratulations, guys," Lance's nephew said, and I pulled him in for a hug.

"You know, if you'd never flaked on him that day, we wouldn't have ever met."

He rubbed the back of his neck and looked embarrassed. He'd grown since then and was now in college studying some tech degree I didn't understand. "I'm glad it worked out. Welcome to the family."

"Thank you." I squeezed his arm and moved to the next outstretched hand.

When we were finally at the last of the chairs we turned around again and raised our still bound hands to everyone, then led our guests toward the clearing where the reception would be held. "Wow," Lance breathed out as we entered the area. It was lined with trees, and as we'd seen earlier, ribbons and streamers were hung from the trees and the poles that held the strings of lights.

"It looks like something out of a fairytale," I said, and Lance immediately looked at me before laughing.

"It is magical. Come on, Prince Charming, let's go see if there's anything we need to do."

"Not today you don't," Joseph said from right behind us. "I told you we were taking care of it, and we are. Go sit down and have a drink. It's nearly time to eat." He rushed off to where the food was being set up before it would be served. We'd talked about this, and he insisted this was best. He had everything he needed, so we let him lead.

"Your table, gentlemen." A waiter I didn't recognize guided us to the table at the front of where the other tables were placed. From here we could see everyone, and for a moment we just sat and watched as our guests were guided to their seats.

A tray of the appetizers we'd helped prep the day before was placed on our table, along with a selection of beer and wine in a metal bucket filled with ice. "It's beautiful," I murmured.

"Not as beautiful as my husband," Lance said, and kissed my cheek. "Thank you for all this, Billie. Without you none of it would have happened."

"Baby, we both helped."

"I don't just mean yesterday, or any of the days this week. It has been a long week already though, not gonna lie. What I mean is if we hadn't met this wouldn't have happened. I wonder what the odds are of a guy from Sacramento ending up in my little eastern town, and him being the most perfect person in the whole world for me."

His ring shone on his finger as he settled his hand on his chin while he smiled at me. "I'd like to think that if we hadn't met then we would have eventually. Fate wasn't going to let us get away from each other." He'd said this many times over the years we'd been together, and looking at him right now, I had to agree. He smiled a watery smile at me and reached to cradle my cheek in his hand. "I love you so much. You're my heart," he whispered so low I had to strain to hear.

"I love you more. You're all I'll ever need," I said back, and I rested my hand over his.

"Okay, lads, eat up. There's a band showing up shortly," Joseph said, and walked away after setting down a shot of leek soup and a round of sourdough bread for us.

"Later," Lance said, and I kissed the palm of his hand while trying to tell myself I could wait to be alone with him.

Thirty-One
Finally Complete

LANCE

We were married. It was so surreal, but as the evening played out in front of me, I knew it was true, and I couldn't have been happier. Ryan danced slowly next to us with Gerald, both lost in a quiet conversation that should have happened years ago.

"Remember, that'll be us," Billie whispered next to my ear as his lips glided along my jaw.

"It already is us. I plan on living a long and happy life with you, Mr. Karl." I glided my hands down his back and ignored the fact we were both still wearing our kilts. It wouldn't take much effort to sneak off into the woods surrounding the park, but I wanted more with Billie than just to get off. I wanted to take time and make love with my husband.

He leaned back enough to meet my eyes. "Good, because I'm not going anywhere, and neither are you by the way. I'm quite happy with what we have, and I don't want anything to change. You really are my heart, and you have my heart, all of it."

"How's it going, lads?" Joseph asked.

"It's been the best day of our lives. Thank you so much for all you've done. None of this would have been possible without you," I said and squeezed his shoulder.

"It's been a pleasure getting to know the two of you. And I have to admit I've been curious about the relatives across the pond. We've been talking, and a few of us are going to come to visit you. It may not be anytime soon, but we'd all really like to keep in touch." A few of his family gathered behind him, all of them smiling and looking between Billie and me.

"You'd better. You know I'll put you to work though. There's plenty of lobster rolls that need making. Not to mention the lobster tacos and loaded fries."

"And tots," Billie added.

"Yeah, you heard him. We'd love for you to visit." I pulled Billie close and kissed his head.

"Well, if you're going to work while you're there, you know I can always use some help," Mom piped up and they all laughed. "You think I'm joking but I'm not." She patted Billie's cheek and walked over to one more table to visit either another relative or a new friend, I wasn't sure.

"She's really not," I whispered, and the fact she turned back to look at me made me think she'd heard me.

"Hey, why don't we switch the menu at our restaurant to Joseph's while he's there. It could be fun, and I think the locals would love it as much as we have," Billie said with a shrug.

"That's a great idea. We'll need to have some advance warning so we can plan it, but I like it." I kissed Billie's cheek, and Joseph smiled at the two of us.

"You two really got it bad," he said for what had to be the hundredth time.

"Yeah, we do." Billie and I both grinned at each other and I pulled him closer to me.

"How long before you're leaving?"

"We'll be here a few more days. Neither of us is ready to leave yet," Billie said.

"I'd love for you to return again. It's truly been a pleasure getting to know the both of you. I never thought I'd meet one of the relatives that had journeyed across the sea all those years ago. And I'm so proud to call both of you, my nephews." He was so sincere, and when Mom walked up, she hugged me from the side Billie wasn't already tucked into.

"Joseph, if you keep it up, you'll have the two of them in tears again," she said.

"Again?" I asked.

"The toast." She squeezed me a little tighter.

"How was I supposed to know Joseph was going to say all that?" I looked between him and my mom while the two of them grinned.

"I may be a man of few words, but when it comes down to telling someone how I feel, I won't shy away from that." His speech was beautiful and spoke of old traditions meeting modern times, and how two hearts that are meant to find each other will. No matter what obstacles are put between them. Even if it's a whole country.

"It was amazing, and since we've mostly talked about food, I was really impressed," Billie said, and then ducked a swat from Joseph.

"Watch it there," Joseph said, and the four of us chatted a while longer before he had to run off to make sure the food was being taken care of. When the song was ending Ryan walked over to us with Gerald next to him.

"Will you be leaving soon?" he asked.

"Yes, but we'll be here a few more days before we leave. The business won't run itself." He smiled at me, but there was sadness there.

"You boys may not know it, but you made a difference to an old man while you were here. Well, two old men. Gerald has been very close to my heart for years, but I just couldn't seem to make myself go and talk to him. Thank you for taking me to the castle that day. If you hadn't asked me, I may never have gone. And we may never have gotten a second chance." He turned to Gerald who was looking at him with so much affection I couldn't help but smile back.

"We're happy to hear that. It's obvious you two need to spend more time together," Billie said. "Thanks again for the recommendation." He held his hand up and wiggled his fingers showing off the shiny new ring he now wore. My ring.

"We'll never forget you, and if you ever decide to cross the pond you'd better stop and visit."

"That we will, Lance, that we will." Gerald took Ryan's hand and the two of them strolled off to their table.

The sound of a tinkling glass got everyone's attention, and I was surprised to see Mom standing in front of the band holding a wine glass and tapping it with a knife. "Everyone, if I could have your attention, please."

"What's going on?" Billie asked.

"No clue," I said, and the two of us sat back down at our table. A selection of wines had been set out and a fresh choice of beers had been added to the metal tub.

"Now most of you know me and for those of you that don't, I'm Alice Karl. I wanted to take this time to propose a toast. Many of you have just recently met Lance and his lovely husband Billie, thank you for making them feel so welcome and loved. Thank you for showing them what our family has been for generations, and for welcoming them into your circle so warmly. And now, because I know you're all ready for a drink,"—she raised her glass—"to Lance and Billie, may they forever love each other the way they do now."

Cheers and shouts of salute rumbled through all of those gathered around us. "I love you, Lance Karl. I think a part of me always loved you even before we met. Thank you so much for this wonderful life." He held his glass out and waited for me.

"You're the one I've been waiting my whole life for," I whispered before our lips met. "I love you, and I can't wait to show you how much." He groaned and rested his forehead against mine.

"Do you think Ian would mind if we wore the kilts back to the hotel?" Billie asked, and I winked. Anything he wanted I'd do my best to get, and anything he needed I'd provide. He was the other half of me, and the only person who would hold my heart.

Several hours, and several toasts later, we were in our room. Billie stood before me still wearing his kilt and nothing else.

"Ye make a striking highlander," I said in my best-worst Irish or possibly Scottish accent. Billie lowered his eyes and walked around the side of the bed.

"What will we be doing on our wedding night, Mr. Karl?" he said in a fantastic Irish accent.

"When did you get so good—" My words were cut off by his kiss as he wasted no time in claiming all of me for his own. His hands glided up my legs to find me hard underneath my kilt. There were definitely advantages to them.

In a flash he rolled me over and flipped up the back of the kilt, so my ass was there for him to do whatever he wanted. And he wanted. "Such a fine, sweet ass," he continued in the same accent. Getting a grip on each cheek, he spread me wide before tasting me.

Fisting the sheets, I fought for control I knew he'd take away from me with the swipe of his tongue. But instead, he blew across my skin, surprising me. I had just relaxed when he licked me, making me flinch and groan. Instantly wanting more. He took his time, making me want him more and more with each second that passed, until I was sure I was going to lose my mind with want for him.

He knew my body so well, and knew exactly how far to push me, and when I nearly fell over the edge, he pulled back. "You ready, baby?" he groaned in my ear, his voice husky and deep.

Unable to answer, I nodded and gripped the sheets even tighter as he pulled my hips up enough to allow him to press his dick against my hole. But he wasn't done with me yet, he slowly slid in just a fraction before sliding back out. He repeated this over and over again, going just a little deeper each time until finally he filled me.

Then he moved. His hips pounded into me before he lifted my body and held me close to his chest. "We're married now, and I will never want anyone the way I want you. My husband, my lover, my very best friend," he whispered while reaching around to grip my straining erection. A few pumps of his hand were all it took for me to spill. Convulsing in the throw of an orgasm so full of passion I wasn't sure I'd survive another, but more than willing to try.

Epilogue
Home

BILLIE

There wasn't a day that went by that I didn't think about our wedding. The way our families had come together for us so far away, and all the love they'd shown us. Now, almost a year later, Lance and I sat at the airport waiting for Joseph to arrive.

"Do you think his plane is late?" Lance asked even though the screen just above his head said it was on time.

"He'll be here any—"

"There they are." Joseph's voice boomed through the airport making both of us smile. He rushed up and lifted first me and then Lance in a crushing hug. Annie hurried to hug us both before telling us how much she'd missed us. It was then I noticed Ryan and Gerald waiting patiently behind them.

"Ryan? It's so good to see you. You too, Gerald." I rushed to hug each of them too, but without as much crushing as I'd endured from Joseph.

"Thanks, I hope you don't mind. When Joseph said he was coming to visit, the two of us thought this was a good time to come here and see some of the sights," Ryan explained, and I grinned as Gerald settled his hand on his lower back.

"The museum let you have time off?"

"Reluctantly," Gerald said, and grinned. "They knew if they said no, I'd tell them I was retiring, and they'd rather that not happen too soon."

"I keep telling him if he retires then we can go see even more of the historical sites we both love. But he does love working at the castle," Ryan said.

"Come on, lads, I want to see the restaurant," Joseph said and glanced toward the door.

"How's married life treating you?" Gerald took Ryan's suitcase and wheeled it along with his own.

"It's great, I think it had to be the perfect start we had." I looked at the four of them and wondered if they really understood how much their kindness and ability to make us feel welcome had meant to us. "We're so happy you've come to visit. Ryan and Gerald, I never would have guessed you'd make the journey, but I'm really so glad you did."

We chatted the whole way to the restaurant and Ryan and Gerald asked question after question about the history of the area and how it had changed from being a small fishing town, to being a big tourist area. "They love the old town area, and down by the docks. When the tall ships are here it draws people from all over the country." Lance pointed out the different areas as we drove by them while our four Irish visitors took in all they could from the car.

"Can we come back to this area and walk around a bit? There's a bakery along the way that looks promising," Joseph said.

"We can do whatever you want." Lance pulled behind the restaurant where we always parked close to both the business and our apartment. "We can leave your luggage for now. After we get you something to eat, I'll drive you to your hotel."

"After that flight we'll all be going to bed early." Joseph stretched before shaking himself out.

"It is a long trip. But totally worth it." Lance led us all along the side of the building. We'd made sure we entered on the other end of the alley, so they didn't see the restaurant until now. There, parked out front, was the bright green food truck with the giant lobster that matched the one we'd incorporated along the side of the building. Lance threw his arms out wide. "Welcome to Lance's Lobster Rolls."

"Well, you didn't tell me you had a giant lobster on the building that matches the one on the roof of your food truck." Joseph slapped him on the back before hurrying over to look at both of them closer. Inside were all of the relatives and friends who were able to be here to welcome them.

"Joseph, get in here and get to work," Lance's mom called from the front door.

Joseph rushed to her and picked her up in a big hug. "Alice, how're you doing?"

"I'm doing great, now come on in, Annie, you too. Ryan and Gerald, there're people here who want to meet you all." Lance and I walked in behind the four of them and watched as they laughed and caught up with people they'd met at our wedding, and others who were new. After everyone was settled at a table and had been fed, we chatted about the past year.

"So much has changed. The business has really taken off. We're actually looking into a second location." I was so proud of everything Lance and I had accomplished. I was still worried about whether we'd be able to handle one more business, but if anyone could make it work it would be us.

"You boys are hard workers, and you deserve everything you've worked so hard for," Dad said as he walked in the door behind us. My family were better about visiting now. It had only been a year, but this was their second visit. "Hey, you didn't think we'd miss out on seeing our long-lost, newly found Irish relatives, did you?" He pulled Joseph in for a hug, and I was reminded how well the two of them got along. Which said a lot because my dad was not easy to deal with. He was driven so much by his business and keeping it going, which was part of the reason I'd ended up here. But he was trying, and for now that was enough.

"Everything okay?" Lance whispered to me while pulling me to his side. His breath on my ear reminded me how close he was, but I didn't need a reminder of how much he cared.

"Everything is perfect. I couldn't have ever imagined a more wonderful life. Or a better person to spend it with."

"Well good thing because I have no intention of ever letting you go." He held me close a moment longer, just enough to let me know he meant every word even though I already knew.

"You've given me everything I could have ever wanted," I whispered to him.

His eyes sparkled as they met mine, and I knew he was thinking the same thing I was. We were the luckiest two guys to ever run into each other while working at a food truck.

"So, will we be working in the food truck while I'm here?" Joseph asked, bringing us back to the present.

"I wanted to ask you about that. It's the Tall Ships Festival this weekend. I was thinking we could make it a family affair this year," Lance said, and laughed when Joseph punched at the air. "So, that's a yes?"

"Oh, it's a hell yes."

"Good thing because we're going to be in two locations this year. The truck and a booth."

"Lance, you're a man after my heart. You know I can't wait to work in the truck," Joseph said with a good amount of excitement in his voice, and a shake of Lance's shoulders.

"Did you say the tall ships will be here?" Gerald asked, making us all laugh.

Lance knew Ryan and Gerald would love the historical part of the event, which was one more reason we'd chosen this time of year for their visit. "We aim to please. Sounds like there's something for everyone while you're here.

"You're all invited to my restaurant too," Alice said. "I've arranged for a historian to take you on a tour of the lighthouse and the grounds." She patted Ryan's hand while she spoke.

"This is going to be the best vacation ever," Joseph said his accent heavy and his eyes full of happiness as he pulled Annie in for a hug.

"No, that was last year. When I married my husband in front of everyone who matters to us. Nothing could ever hold a candle to that," Lance whispered before kissing my cheek.

"Oh god, you two are just as bad now as you were then," Joseph said, but smiled as he shook his head.

"Yeah, we are." I turned to my husband then and kissed him. My heart did that funny little flutter it did every time he held me, and I knew without a doubt even if he never said the words again, he'd love me as much as I'd always love him.

THE END

About the Author

BL Maxwell grew up in a small town listening to her grandfather spin tales about his childhood. Later she became an avid reader and after a certain vampire series she became obsessed with fanfiction. She soon discovered Slash fanfiction and later discovered the MM genre and was hooked. Many years later, she decided to take the plunge and write down some of the stories that seem to run through her head late at night when she's trying to sleep.

Contact:

Email: blmaxwell.writer@gmail.com
   https://smart.bio/blmaxwellwriter/

Other Books By BL Maxwell

Thank you for reading Brown Eyed Boy.
Green Eyed Boy, Lobster Tales Book One, is available Here:
https://mybook.to/GreenEyedBoy

**Two strangers, drawn together over their work ethic,
and sealing the deal over delicious lobster rolls. They
could just be the perfect match.**
After quitting his job, Billie Watts hits all the food festivals he
can as he drives across the country. When he finally reaches
Stoney Brook, Maine, he's excited to find he's there just in
time to try one of the lobster rolls he's heard so much about.
The bright neon yellow food truck with a giant red lobster on
top looks like the perfect place to try it.
Lance Karl is as ready as he can be for the start of the
three-day Tall Ships Festival and hopes to sell enough lobster
rolls out of his food truck to make a good start towards owning
a restaurant. The day begins cold and misty, and a text from
his nephew saying he can't help him is not the perfect start
he'd hoped for.
When a green-eyed stranger interrupts his frantic morning,
Lance doesn't realize meeting Billie will not only change his
day, but maybe even the rest of his life. Two strangers, drawn
together over their work ethic, and sealing the deal over delicious lobster rolls. They could just be the perfect match. A
small-town MM Vacation romance.#friends to lovers #meet-
cute #workplace romance #mm romance

Enjoy a Free copy of Try To Remember. A short story with Andy and Link.
https://blmaxwellwriter.com/free-reads/
And a Free copy of A Night To Remember. A short story with Sam and Erik.
https://books2read.com/u/baDrw8

Preorder The Things We Lose: https://my-book.to/TTWLose

BETTER TOGETHER series

Better Together
Chains Required
The First Twelve
The Better Together Boxset

THE STONE series

Stone Under Skin
Blood Beneath Stone
Stone Hearts
The Stone Series Box Set

SMALL TOWN CITY series

Remember When
A Night to Remember (Short Story)

Try To Forget
Try To Remember (Short Story)
One Last Chance

CONSORTIUM TRILOGY

Burning Addiction
Freezing Aversion

VALLEY GHOSTS series

Ghost Hunted
Ghost Haunted
Ghost Trapped
Ghost Hexed
Ghost Handled
Ghost Shadow
Haunting Destiny

FOUR PACKS Trilogy

The Slow Death
The Ultimate Sacrifice
The Final Salvation

STANDALONE

The List
Double Black Diamonds
Ride: The Chance of a Lifetime
Check Yes or No
A Ghost of a Chance
Tutu

Salt & Lime
Amos Ridge
Six Months
Ten or Fifteen Miles
The Snake in the Castle
Green Eyed Boy
A Beach Far Away
The Things We Find
Blinding Light
Peppermint Mocha Kisses

Small Town City Series

Remember When
BL Maxwell
https://mybook.to/RememberWhenA
A night to remember, a confession, and a lifetime of love in
this small town, friends to lovers Christmas romance.
Andrew Lawson's life in Sacramento has turned from being
everything he dreamed of growing up, to a lonely place where
finding someone special to share his life with is impossi-
ble. When the first person he meets on returning home for
Thanksgiving is his childhood friend Link, it's a reminder
of happier times when his whole future lay in front of him.
Agreeing to a drink before heading to his parent's place is a
way to reconnect, and a great way to start the holiday.
Link Stanton never considered leaving the small farming town
he grew up in, but he misses Andy more than he'll ever admit.
Secretly lusting after a friend is bad enough but being in love
with him is so much worse. One drink with friends seems
harmless enough, after all, catching up on old times can't be a
bad thing, until beers turn to shots, and Link reveals how he
really feels.
Everything could change, and if Andrew doesn't remember
Link's heartfelt confession, they could carry on as friends. But,

if he does remember, this could be either the worst, or the best, Christmas of all. #smalltownromance #Holidayromance #mmromance #Christmas #friendstolovers

Try To Forget
BL Maxwell
https://mybook.to/TryToForget
After being dumped by his boyfriend, spending the weekend alone wasn't something Sam Braun was looking forward to. So, when the hairstylist that works next to his bookstore invites him to his hometown for the weekend, Sam jumps at the chance. Visiting the small town of Occident could be just what he needs to forget, at least for a few days.
Erik Thorne has lived his whole life in the same town where nothing new ever happens, and any stranger who comes to town is always a big deal. When his old friend Andy brings a friend home for the weekend, Erik is drawn to the man in a way that confuses him at first. But his curiosity about the gorgeous blond from the city gets the better of him, and he can't resist spending more time with him.
Sam was hoping to forget his troubles when he meets Erik. While Erik can't seem to think of anything besides the city boy with the bookstore he can't wait to visit. Distance might not be the only thing that stands between them, as they find out admitting what you want isn't always easy. Each book can be read as a standalone. #AgeGap, #MMRomance, #FriendsToLovers #OppositesAttract #SmallTownRomance #City/Country
One Last Chance (New Release)
BL Maxwell
https://mybook.to/OLCSmalltown
Stu Lawson had always lived in the small town of Occident. He'd been born a farmer, and he was more than happy to stay a farmer even when his dad decided it wasn't the life for him. He's been raising his daughter since the day she was born,

and he's never regretted being a single dad, but Stu has a few secrets.

Morgan Grant was born into a life he never wanted and had done everything he could to avoid. Staying drunk helps him forget and numbs the pain he can't bring himself to face. After a long night of drinking, he ends up dumped in a small town north of Sacramento without money, his phone, or a way to get back to the city he calls home.

Stu's focus has always been his daughter, but he can't control his curiosity about the stranger who shows up in Occident alone in the middle of the night. He offers to help, even when he knows he shouldn't. Old feelings rise to the surface and he's helpless to ignore them, or Morgan. This stranger could be his chance at happiness, or his downfall. #singledad #gayromance #stranded #smalltownromance #secrets

Haunting Destiny

A Valley Ghosts Christmas
https://mybook.to/HauntingDestinyA
Series Link: mybook.to/ValleyGhostsSeries
It's Christmas, and an invitation to a party is too tempting for Wade and Jason to pass up. When The Running Scared Paranormal Research crew realize it's not just a party but a gathering of all the paranormal investigators in the area, they're suspicious but excited to meet others in their same business. A mystery, a ghost, and a love story play out for them through the evening onboard the riverboat docked in Old Sacramento where the party is held.

After the party, Wade and Jason decide to take a big step in their relationship. One they've both wanted for years, but never seemed to find the perfect time for. In a spur of the moment decision, they decide to go for it, and even a snowstorm won't stop them from getting married. With the help of all-wheel drive, Santa, and a ghost, they'll get their happy ending. (Can be read as a standalone) #FriendsToLovers #Ghosts #Ghosthunters #PNR #MMRomance #Secret Wedding #HolidayRomance

Peppermint Mocha Kisses

https://mybook.to/PeppermintMK
Randy Miller wants nothing more than to make a living selling the fantastic cookies he dreams up when he's not working as a web designer. He's always loved baking, but he's afraid of taking the leap from hobby to business. Mostly he's afraid of failing, and of Eli coming up with a better recipe.
Eli Canton has a crush. A big crush on someone who avoids him whenever he can. Eli loves everything about Randy, even if he's grouchy and seems to work way too much. Eli knows he's not all bad and hopes to have a chance with him someday. A broken oven throws the two of them together, and even though Randy doesn't want to admit it, he likes the time he spends with Eli. And Eli definitely can't wait to spend more time with Randy. Now if only they can make it past the annual cookie exchange and possibly Valentine's Day to their own sweet happy ending. #smalltown Romance, #opposites attract, #MM Romance

Milton Keynes UK
Ingram Content Group UK Ltd.
UKHW010803150823
426904UK00004B/256

9 798223 693413